PAUL WEAVER AND THE SOUL REAVER

S.C. McMurray

ISBN: 9781963832143 (paperback) / 9781963832280 (ebook)
LCCN: 2025933040
Copyright © 2025 by S. C. McMurray
Cover illustration © 2025 by Kyle Newsock
Interior illustrations © 2025 by Kyle Newsock

Printed in the United States of America.

Names, characters, and incidents depicted in this book are products of the author's imagination or are used fictitiously. Any resemblance to actual events, locales, organizations, or persons, living or dead, is entirely coincidental and beyond the intent of the author or the publisher.

All rights reserved. No part of this book may be reproduced or transmitted in any form or by any means, electronic or mechanical, including photocopying, recording or by any information storage or retrieval system without written permission of the publisher, except for the inclusion of brief quotations in a review.

NO AI TRAINING: Without in any way limiting the author's [and publisher's] exclusive rights under copyright, any use of this publication to "train" generative artificial intelligence (AI) technologies to generate text is expressly prohibited. The author reserves all rights to license uses of this work for generative AI training and development of machine learning language models.

Kinkajou Press
9 Mockingbird Hill Rd
Tijeras, New Mexico 87059
info@kinkajoupress.com
www.kinkajoupress.com

Dedication

For Kelsey, Kaelin, and Jase.

Ep. 29: I can't believe it's come to this.
Knighthood Never Looked So Good - 5,008 Views

I'm going to steal my principal's soul.

I get it. It sounds crazy and definitely evil. Don't get the wrong impression about me, though. I'm not crazy or evil, though there is crazy *and* evil in this story.

I'm just a concerned citizen. And I didn't come to this decision lightly. I came to this decision *heavily* because someone I care about is in danger. Like for real danger. Like the forever-dead-as-a-door-nail kind of danger.

And I have to help him.

If you're new to my channel, you're probably wondering what my principal did that led to this drastic decision. Well, I don't have time to recap now, so you'll have to watch my previous uploads.

Whether you watch the videos or not, wish me luck. I'm gonna need it.

If I pull it off, you'll know, because I'll be right here posting another video.

And if you don't see me again... Well, I guess you know what that means.

This is Paladin Knight-in-Training, Paul Weaver, signing off.

The Sixth Grade Series

Ep. 1: Do You Smell That?
Knighthood Never Looked So Good - 113 Views

Well, I'm ba—Hold on. Let me adjust my camera.

That's better.

Welcome to the newest season of "Knighthood never look so Good". Name's Paul and I'm documenting my daily adventures as a Paladin Knight-in-Training.

It's been a while. Too long some might say. So long in fact, I think I've got facial hair!

Never mind. That's just barbecue sauce from the chicken nuggets I ate on the way home from camp. Yum!

Speaking of camp. It was a lot more fun than I expected. I guess Mom and Dad were right about that. We did a lot of cool stuff and I met some fun people, but also some really smelly people. That's a weird thing to say but I'm not kidding. In all my journeys as a Paladin Knight-in-Training, I don't think I've encountered such stench. There was a whole cabin of kids who stank worse than Samwise when he got skunked last summer.

What? Don't look at me like that, Samwise. You stank horribly.

If you're new to my channel, Samwise is my corgi. Who I just offended apparently because he left the room. If you've never seen a corgi before, they're adorable little dogs with thick bodies and big ears that stand straight up when they're excited. At least Samwise's do. Most corgis I've seen are one solid color, like red or black, but Samwise is a tri-color corgi with mostly brown and black fur, except for a strip of white between his eyes and a white belly.

That sound you may have heard was his tiny toenails clicking across my bedroom floor. Don't worry about him. He'll get over it. Samwise is loyal like his namesake from *The Lord of the Rings*. Besides I wasn't lying. If you've ever had a dog get skunked, you know what I mean. Yuck.

Those kids smelled like that too. I don't think they showered at all. They were proud of it. They said it was girl repellent. It worked. Not even the lady counselors would go near them. That said, they were cool and fun to hang out with, as long as you brought a clothespin with you. I told them about my channel here on Fantasy-Tube where I'm documenting my quest to become a Paladin Knight. I'm up to 113 subscribers, so some of the kids from camp may be watching. If you're one of them, I hope your moms didn't keel over dead from the stench when you got home. And thanks for the parting gift. The stink bomb will be a nice potion to add to my arsenal.

Camp was fun and everything, but that's not really what I want to talk about. Ever since I got home, something has felt… off. My parents are still my parents. You know, working at their law firm all the time doing legal stuff or whatever. My pappaw has to live in a nursing home for a while because he fell while I was at camp, so it's quieter around here with him not popping in to visit. But that's not it. It's my sister, Ruth.

She's been… different. Mom and Dad say it's because she just got her license and she's "expressing her independence."

I don't understand how getting her license makes her like George Washington. I don't remember him driving a Honda Civic across the Delaware River. All I know is something about my sister has changed. For example, me and her have a tradition that the night before the first day of school, we flush ice cubes down the toilet in hopes of conjuring future snow days.

Wait!

She's home!

You guys should meet her.

Hey, Ruth!

What?

You should come in here.

I don't have time for one of your videos. My car is running downstairs.

Running? Like a marathon? If so, I hope it gets first place.

I'm not in the mood, Paul.

Okay. Okay. Just don't forget about the ice cubes in the toilet.

Yeah. Don't count on it.

What? Last year it worked! It was a good thing!

Well, good things change, Paul.

Do they have to?

Okay… She ignored me.

I don't get it. She was the one who showed me the spell to begin with. And last year it worked. We flushed a whole tray—eight jumbo ice cubes—down the toilet and a massive snowstorm knocked us out of school for almost two weeks in February. Two weeks! That's like an extra Christmas break! But I guess this year I'm all on my own.

If any of my fellow Fantasy-Tubers have faced this situation before, I would accept any tips on how to stop Ruth from going all George Washington on me.

I gotta go. I got some ice cubes to flush. Fingers crossed the spell still works with me flying solo.

Ep. 2: The First Day of School Blues

Knighthood Never Looked So Good - 156 Views

Well, my first day of sixth grade didn't go as well as I hoped.

I have all the mean teachers.

The sisters of Medusa, their snakeheads hidden by their poofy dyed hair.

No one dared move or say a word all day. Ms. Hefflestine's Math class was all numbers and figures, no real problem solving. Mrs. Blotter's Science class could've really used one of those small chemical explosions you see in movies just to spice things up. Mrs. Paneli's silent reading was truly silent reading. As my pappaw likes to say, it was so quiet in my classroom you could hear a mouse fart.

The only class that was fun was Social Studies, taught by Mr. Macadoo. He's new this year and he looks kind of like Kylo Ren from the new *Star Wars* movies—only with glasses and a chain necklace and no cape—which is fitting since his classroom is decorated with *Star Wars* posters. I think he may secretly be a fantasy fan like us, maybe even a Paladin Knight!

What really made my day bad was lunch—and I don't even mean the soggy hamburger. I usually sit with my best friend and fellow Paladin Knight-in-Training, Hurston Flores, but he sat with a new kid at the popular table. If our school didn't have this stupid rule about only letting seven students sit at a table, I would have tried to sit with them, but they were full so I sat alone.

Tomorrow, I may sneak Samwise into school so I have someone to talk to during lunch.

Do you think a corgi would fit in a book bag?

Ep. 3: Flying Solo(but not with Han Solo)

Knighthood Never Looked So Good - 199 Views

Friday during the first part of the school year is usually my favorite day of the week for one simple reason: Friday night football games!

Football's not really my thing, but the whole town assembles at our school's football field to watch the boys of Twin Valley High battle on the gridiron—except Hurston and me... usually. Home football games turn Twin Valley into a ghost town, leaving us the freedom to explore our town's secrets without fear of being chased off somebody's property with an angry broom—or worse. And this Friday I had something really good for us to investigate.

I tracked down Hurston at recess to give him the invite. We don't have any classes together this year, so lunch and recess are all I got. He was playing basketball with the new kid, who I do have a class with—Math—and some of the other guys from the popular table.

I was like, "The first game of the season's tonight."

Hurston wouldn't meet my eyes and looked at the ground. All he said was, "Yeah. I know."

I reminded him about that one time on the bus when the older kids told us there was a treasure hidden in the Swafford's old place and then hit him with the awesome news: "The fire department finally burned the old house down. It's nothing but ash now. We need to go down there and check it out. See what we can find!"

Was Hurston excited about that? No! He kinda just went quiet and stuck his hands in his pockets and was all "Ummm... sounds fun but... ummm... I already have plans tonight."

I tried to hide my disappointment, but I don't think I did a good job of it because Hurston looked down at the ground again when he told me the new kid, Levi, invited him to go with him and some other guys to the game.

You know something's going on when people won't look you in the eye. At least that's what my pappaw says.

Anyway, I was like, "Oh. Okay. Maybe we can hang out tomorrow or something?"

And he just shrugged and said, "I'll call you," and then he jogged back to the court to play basketball.

Something tells me he isn't going to call.

Since Hurston is out, I decided to ask Ruth if she wanted to come, but she was gone before I got the chance. Which means it's just you and me, Samwise.

You'll go with me, won't ya boy?

If he could talk, he'd say, "All the way to the fires of Mount Doom."

This is Paladin Knight-in-Training, Paul Weaver, and my trusty companion, Samwise, signing off. I'll let you know what we find at the Swafford's old place.

Ep. 4: Holy—- I don't like to cuss —-that was crazy! Knighthood Never Looked So Good - 316 Views

I have to whisper because my parents just got home and if they catch me recording a video this late, they'll take away my laptop again.

I was going to wait until the morning to tell you guys, but I'm too excited. No. Excited's not the right word. Scared? No. Not that either. I don't know what the right word is. All I can say is I'm something between excited and scared because my heart is still pounding and I have to tell someone what happened.

So, after dinner when my parents went back to the office and Ruth was supposed to be watching me, Samwise and I set out for the Swafford's old place. With Samwise riding in my parents' old bike stroller behind me, I rode my bike all the way to the edge of town. The roads were deserted, but the lights of the football field glowed on the horizon and the marching band played in the distance.

As I got closer to my destination, the scent of ash on the air made my nose bristle. I thought at first that the fire must still be going and expected to see roaring flames once we reached our destination, but the firefighters did a good job because the fire was all put out when we got there.

Samwise and I ducked under the caution tape. Well, not Samwise. He doesn't really have to duck under anything—the benefit of having short stubby legs. I don't know if us being there was illegal. I didn't see a No Trespassing sign. But don't tell my mom or the police just in case.

Anyway, we poked around a little. I was hoping to discover a treasure, like a magical ring that turns its wearer invisible, but all I found was the remnants of an old recliner and a few metal clothes hangers.

The thing is, the smell of ash still hung in the air and we couldn't figure out why because it smelled different than that old smoky recliner. The air smelled sort of like my pappaw's cigars only much stronger.

We were about to leave when I heard something coming from the woods behind us. Samwise heard it too. His ears perked up and his body went all still. I sucked in a breath and listened. Over the chirping of the evening crickets came the melody of someone singing or... chanting. It was a strange kind of song in a language I didn't understand.

Samwise had that determined look in his eyes and I knew what he was going to do.

I shook my head and whispered, "Don't do it, Sam. Don't."

But of course, he did. Like a rocket shooting to the moon, he bolted into the woods toward the sound.

I won't lie to you guys, I wasn't exactly thrilled about going in there. The woods were thick with honeysuckle and poison ivy and it was getting dark. But I couldn't let my dog venture into the woods all alone. What kind of Paladin Knight-in-Training would I be if I did that?

So, I went in after him. Though the gloom pressed against me, there was just enough light to see the white fur of his heart-shaped butt bouncing up and down as he maneuvered through the thicket and bounded over the fallen tree limbs.

He stopped at a clump of ivy-covered maple trees. That cigar smell reeked there. I knelt next to Samwise and was about to give him an earful when the chanting stopped. But not just the chanting, the insects too.

Pure silence.

The sisters of Medusa would've liked it. But I sure didn't. I shivered though it was still hot outside. Samwise let out a tiny whimper and pressed himself against me as he peered forward at something.

Beyond the clump of trees lay a small clearing. Someone or something moved through the yellowing grass like Bigfoot in one of those Bigfoot hunting shows my dad likes to stream. I told Samwise not to make a sound, then I inched forward. The thistles scratched my legs and a thorny bush stabbed my arms, so I climbed one of the maple trees and crawled along a sturdy branch.

I now had a pretty good view of the clearing and what I saw made me shiver again.

It wasn't Bigfoot—unless Bigfoot wears a ratty old bathrobe—but some tall man or woman standing before a pile of rocks. A fire danced atop of the stone altar, spewing the cigar smelly smoke into the air. The stranger bowed their head before it, their hooded cloak hiding their face. They stood completely still with a thick leather-bound book in their hands.

But they weren't reading it, just holding it.

After a couple of seconds, the person in the hooded cloak lifted their head and began chanting again.

It sounded something like this:

"THISS DA MISH DA THAVA ZIMA HA."

The person kept repeating it, getting louder each time.

"THISS DA MISH DA THAVA ZIMA HA!"

"THISS DA MISH DA THAVA ZIMA HA!"

"THISS DA MISH DA THAVA ZIMA HA!"

And then something strange happened that I... that I can't really explain.

The fire began to change colors. It went from orange to red to blue then purple. Have you ever seen purple fire before? Because I haven't. And the fire also grew larger, like the chants were gasoline.

The fire mesmerized me. I couldn't stop looking at it. I was like Hurston and the lifeguard at the public pool.

Anyway, at that moment, the tree branch I was standing on broke with a snap that echoed out of the woods! I managed to grab hold of another branch as I fell, and I just hung there. Samwise whined and stood up on his hind legs, but there was nothing he could do.

The stranger in the ratty cloak stopped chanting and stomped toward us, the old book clutched against their side. Samwise took a couple steps forward and bent his head low, baring his teeth.

"No Sam," I whispered, "no."

There was no way he was going to let that ratty bathrobe person harm me. But I didn't want them to harm Samwise either. Samwise retreated but kept his gaze locked forward.

Though my hands were all sweaty and I didn't have a great grip on the branch, I decided silence was our best strategy.

The mysterious figure reached the end of the clearing and scanned the woods in front of them. I still couldn't see their face but I caught what looked like a title on the spine of the book.

Abs something and the word *Key.*

I could be wrong. It was written in cursive and I'm not a great reader, or writer for that matter. I get letters and words turned around a lot. Plus, I wasn't real focused on reading. I was focused on not being discovered.

Even though my knuckles were white from me squeezing the branch so hard, my grip was slipping.

Just hold on. Just hold on, I kept thinking.

The figure stood not ten feet away from Samwise and me. Finally, after what felt like an eternity, he or she turned around and headed back toward the fire. I let out a breath I didn't realize I was holding and a bead of sweat drained down from my scalp to the tip of my nose, tickling it. And though I tried to fight it—

"AAHCHOO!"

My sneeze made me lose my grip on the tree branch and I fell to the forest floor, barely missing Samwise.

And here's the scary part.

The figure snapped back around toward us, flashing two glowing white eyes. I kid you not. They were glowing.

The figure stomped toward us. I froze for a second then yelled, "Run, Sam, run!"

And he did and so did I. The two of us moved so fast we were like a couple of spring pigs realizing it's butchering day, as my pappaw likes to say.

Save the bacon!

We reached my bike. I heaved Samwise under my arm and held him on my lap. I couldn't risk him in the stroller. Not looking back, I pedaled as hard as I could toward home.

So now you can see why I'm somewhere between excited and scar—

Knock! Knock!

Are you recording a video in there?

Oh crap! That's my mom. I better go.

Ep. 5: It's not Halloween Makeup
Knighthood Never Looked So Good - 249 Views

I think I know what we may be dealing with here.

I barely slept last night. You know how I said I was somewhere between excited and scared, well after I turned the lights off so I could go to bed, I was definitely favoring one side of that equation.

I kept seeing those white glowing eyes. I kept imagining the figure crossing the lawn, opening our back door, and coming up the stairs to my room as silent as a vampire. I stared at my bedroom door in the dark, the hair on my arms standing up, just waiting for it to creak open.

Samwise just slumbered away, hogging the bed like usual. I have to admit, his snoring made me feel better. People say dogs have a sixth sense about ghosts and stuff so…

But we're not dealing with a ghost here. At least I'm pretty sure we're not. The question of what we're dealing with is why I went to see Pappaw this morning.

Pappaw is the bravest person I know and the wisest. He fought in the Vietnam War, which technically wasn't a war because our government never declared it a war. Instead, they called it a "police action." I'm not sure what that means but, according to Pappaw, calling it a "police action" is a load of hogwash because it sure felt like a war over there.

When he got out of the war, he went to college where he met my mammaw. I never met her—she died of cancer before I was born—but I've seen pictures. She looked like my mom and Ruth, tall and skinny with dark hair and kind green eyes. Pappaw never remarried and my mom still cries at important events like Christmas and stuff because they both miss her a lot which makes me miss her in a way, too, like I lost out on something special.

Anyway, Pappaw is a historian doctor. What I mean is, at the local college where he taught, his students called him Dr. Fishborne—but he can't practice medicine. He does know lots of stuff though and he gives good advice.

Pappaw's the reason I started this channel. He likes hearing my stories and told me I should keep a record of them, like how he kept a journal about his time in Vietnam. I told him I don't like to write because it takes me a long time and I make a bunch of mistakes.

When I told him that, he got all gruff and said, "Hogwash. We live in the 21st century. You don't have to write to keep a journal these days."

He was talking about vlogging. So here I am on Fantasy-Tube.

Because he's a historian doctor, I figured he may know something about the old leather book, *Absa* something *Key*. So, this morning, as Mom sipped coffee and I finished a bowl of Cinnamon Toast Crunch, I said to Mom, "Can we go see Pappaw today?"

Pappaw only lives a few miles away, and I usually ride my bike there, but because he fell this summer and broke his hip, he's in a nursing home in the next town over.

Mom stirred her coffee with this disappointed look and was like, "I'd love to, but I can't. The Jones Case is about to go to trial and your father and I have a lot to get done. Sorry bud."

I reminded her that she and Dad have been working on that case forever and after drinking the cinnamon-y remainder of my milk, demanded to know what Indiana Jones did this time to get in trouble?

Mom chuckled and said it wasn't *Indiana Jones* but something about this really old mansion known as The Radford Jones Estate. I guess she and Dad are representing a longtime maid who used to work there, but she wouldn't explain any further because it was "too complicated."

I was actually getting curious because that old mansion is kinda fascinating in a creepy haunted house sort of way and countered with, "Like trying-to-find-the-Ark-of-the-Covenant complicated?"

Mom laughed in agreement but clarified there were no melting Nazis involved.

If you don't get the reference, she was talking about the movie *Indiana Jones and the Raiders of the Lost Ark* where the Nazi bad guy's face gets melted in the end. It's kinda scary and gory but also awesome! Mom, Dad, Ruth, and me and Samwise binged the movies last spring. Dad was supposed to cover my eyes at that part but he didn't.

Anyway, I asked again about going to see Pappaw. And when Mom narrowed her eyes at me and asked me why, my stomach knotted up because—

If you end up watching this, I'm sorry, Mom.

—because I knew I had to lie to her.

Is there a statue of limitations for lying to your parents? Wait? Is that the right word? Is statue one of those words that sounds the same but has different meanings like but and butt? Probably. And also, can you buy statues on Amazon? I hope so because I told her I wanted to talk to him about camp. Which wasn't a complete lie. I did want to tell him about camp, especially the cabin of smelly kids. But it wasn't the full truth. If I told Mom about what happened last night, she would freak and put me and Samwise on house arrest.

Even with my pleading, Mom said no. The Jones case was just too important.

But then, Ruth came bounding down the stairs, heading for the front door, and Mom smiled with inspiration. Really big like this… then called for my sister.

"Ruth. I need you, dear."

Okay. That's not my best impersonation but still.

I couldn't see Ruth, but I heard her sigh. She wasn't in a good mood. And when she stepped into the entryway to our kitchen, something about her looked different but I couldn't figure out what. She was just as tall as usual. Her hair shrouding her round face.

When Mom asked her to take me to see Pappaw, she crossed her arms and was like, "At the nursing home? For real? But Janae and I are going to the outlet mall and the nursing home is in the opposite direction!"

Her tone must've made Mom mad because she raised her voice a little and pulled out one of the well-worn parent cards when me or Ruth complain about something: "Do I need remind you who paid for that car you're driving?"

Ruth had no comeback. Like I said, that parent card is like a powerful Pokémon attack. So instead, she scrunched her face, glared at me, and gave me two minutes to get ready.

I know Mom wouldn't have let her leave without me, but Ruth looked serious, so I placed my empty cereal bowl into the sink and sprinted upstairs to get dressed.

Ruth was waiting in the car when I got back. I was barely buckled up before she started driving away, scowling.

I don't know why she's been in such a mood lately. When I asked her what was going on, she snapped at me, "Nothing's going on!"

But something definitely was. She even looked different. And after driving for a while in what could be called "tense" silence, I finally saw it. She had something on her face. When I pointed it out, she peered into the rearview mirror in a panic, probably because she thought it was a pimple or something. But it wasn't a pimple. It was Halloween makeup. Or at least that's what I thought so I told her.

She rolled her eyes and corrected me, "It's not Halloween makeup. It's real makeup. Blush and ocean liner."

And when I pointed out that Mom doesn't wear that stuff, she snapped at me again, saying Mom didn't need to in order to look pretty. But the thing is, I don't think Ruth needs to either. And when I told her that, her scowl faded for a while until she said under breath, "I wish that were true."

I don't know why, but that made me feel kind of sad. Like—

Bark! Bark! Bark!

Sorry, that's Samwise. He's outside... barking at something. There's...

I'll be back. I need to check this out.

Ep. 6: Caught by Surprise
Knighthood Never Looked So Good - 199 Views

That was really strange.

Samwise was in our front yard barking. If you watched my last video, you heard that. But it wasn't his usual bark, like when he's chasing squirrels or yapping at the mailwoman. It was deeper, like when he's afraid.

I ran to the window and he was barking at something across the street—an old person's car, like the old ladies at my church drive. But it was maroon with a long front-end, and I don't think I've seen that exact car at St. John's.

I grabbed my binoculars to get a better look at the person in the driver's seat, but they hit the gas and pulled away, peeling out.

I think a man was driving. I didn't see any glowing white eyes so that's a relief. Still, if you happen to live in my neck of the woods and you know someone who drives a maroon old person's car with a long front-end, let me know in the comments.

Anyway, before the creepy car interrupted my last video—I

don't blame Samwise, he was doing what good dogs do—I was saying, I think I know what we are dealing with or at least partly.

After Ruth dropped me off at the nursing home, a nice lady from the front desk led me down a long depressing corridor to Pappaw's room. He was propped up in his bed reading a book. His legs were covered by a white blanket, with a picture of him and my mammaw on the nightstand next to him. It was from some kind of ceremony because he was in his military uniform.

Pappaw was caught up in his book and didn't notice us standing in the doorway, so the lady from the front desk knocked on the doorframe and said, "Dr. Fishborne, you have a visitor."

Pappaw peered up from the pages and his eyes went wide under his thick gray eyebrows as he opened his arms up and gestured for me to give him a hug. I approached him and, though my pappaw is my pappaw, I leaned in from the side because hugging your grandpa in public feels kind of weird, you know?

He squeezed me tight and immediately asked about his other favorite person in the world: Samwise, or as he calls him, "Sammy."

Pappaw is the only one who calls my dog "Sammy" and probably the only person, other than me, who could get away with it. Maybe it's because Pappaw feeds Samwise from the table whenever he comes over for dinner. And if Minecraft has taught me anything, the key to a dog's heart is through his stomach.

I told him I didn't think I was allowed to bring pets in there and Pappaw waved wildly and cried, "Hogwash!" saying Sammy was welcome there anytime.

I promised to bring him next time and he promised to save some scraps from his dinner, but instructed me to keep this arrangement a secret from the nurses. I agreed. I told him about camp and the smelly kids and he told me about how he fell while checking the mail and how he's going to have to be here for a few months. I couldn't believe it!

"A few months?" I said. "Yeesh!" No offense to the nice lady who showed me to his room, but that place seems way boring.

And when I told Pappaw that, he said, "A place is only as boring as you make it," before pointing to his head and adding, "I have my brain, my books, and the memory of your beautiful grandmother, so I have plenty to keep the buzzards away." Which confused me at first because I didn't see any buzzards around. But as he explained, and you probably already figured out, he meant he has plenty to keep him alive.

And by alive, he means learning, because another thing he likes to say is, "The day you stop learning is the day you die."

Which is true if you think about it, because you can't learn anything when you're brain dead.

And that's when I spotted my opportunity to ask about what I saw last night. I had to be careful though, because if he felt I was putting myself in any kind of danger, he'd tell Mom.

So I was like, "You've read lots of old books, right?"

And he was like, "Several, why do you ask? Are you looking for a recommendation?"

And that's when my stomach knotted up again because I had to tell a lie and Paladins are supposed to be honest.

Ignoring the guilt in my stomach, I told him "my friend" had watched a movie that had a strange book in it. Pappaw seemed intrigued and wanted to know more so I glanced toward the door, just to make sure no one was in earshot, and said, "Yeah. In the movie, a guy dressed in a robe stood over a fire with a book, chanting something, and the fire was changing colors."

Pappaw arched one of his bushy eyebrows and I got the impression that he knew more about my situation than he was letting on, because he said, "Is it fair to assume your friend's parents didn't know he was watching this movie?"

It took me a few seconds, but I got his meaning and confirmed it would be safe to assume that, but added, "It would be safe for me to assume my friend would like to keep it that way."

Pappaw was cool with that as long as "my friend" wasn't watching anything that would harm his mind.

He then asked me to describe the book to him, which I did, squinting hard to remember everything about it. "It was old," I told him, "like that fancy Bible printed by that English guy you showed me when we all went to that huge library in Washington D.C. a couple of summers ago."

Of course, the historian doctor had to interrupt me to point out the English guy was John or Jonas Gutenberg, and he was actually German—not English—and the huge library was the Library of Congress, and that Bible was one of the first books mass printed using movable type in the Western World.

Hey. At least I got the Washington D.C. part right.

Anyway, I told Pappaw the book was old like that German guy's Bible and thicker than the mattress he was laying on and the person with the robe wasn't reading from it, just holding it, chanting in some language I couldn't understand.

Pappaw rubbed the gray hair on his chin for a few seconds and then asked if there was anything on the cover, like any drawings or a title. I told him I—I mean—*my friend* didn't see any drawings, just some words written in cursive, that said *Abs* something *Key*.

Pappaw rubbed his chin again, this time for even longer before finally saying what he thought it was: a grimoire.

"A grim what?" I asked. So he spelled it out for me. "G. R. I. M. O. I. R. E. Grimoire," he said, though that spelling seemed like it would sound more like grim-orry.

Pappaw must've noticed the puzzled look on my face because he added, "It's pronounced grim-war."

"Grim-war," I repeated. "Like the war in Vietnam!"

That brought a quick smile to his face and then he explained that a grimoire was a book of spells and potions that often included instructions on how to make magical items. And just when he was about to tell me who he thought the person chanting might have been, someone walked into the room I never expected to see: Mr. Macadoo, my Social Studies teacher.

I was dumbstruck.

It's so awkward bumping into a teacher outside of school. It feels unnatural, like a peanut butter and mayonnaise sandwich.

To make things worse, he was dressed in regular clothes. It was like he was a convict who had escaped prison and traded in his striped prison pajamas for jeans and a t-shirt. The only thing that was recognizable was the gold chain sticking out from his collar.

He'd just got done visiting his grandma in another wing, I guess, and was walking by when he overheard me talking about Vietnam. I was still unable to speak, so Pappaw did all the talking.

When Mr. Macadoo spotted the photo of Pappaw in uniform with my Mammaw, he perked up, nearly jumping out of his HEYDUDEs in excitement and shouting, "You served in the 7th Calvary!"

Pappaw was super impressed and he complemented Mr. Macadoo on his good eye for recognizing the patch on the sleeve of his uniform.

And then Mr. Macadoo did one of the geekiest things a person could do, and that means a lot coming from me. I mean I'm not exactly Tom Holland.

Mr. Macadoo stood up straight, clicked his heels together, saluted, and said, "Then a Garry Owen to you!" Which sent Pappaw grinning from ear to ear because that was the 7th Calvary's old marching tune and slogan.

Then Mr. Macadoo shrugged it off, stating that war history was a passion of his, before thanking Pappaw for his service to our country and making his goodbye.

And to make the awkwardness just a little more awkward, before leaving he turned to me and said, "Paul, I'll see you in class on Monday. Maybe then you'll have something to say," before winking and disappearing down the hall.

Needless to say, it took a while before the awkwardness of bumping into my teacher outside of school went away. But at least it was Mr. Macadoo and not one of Medusa's sisters. Yuck! I probably would've turned to stone right there. And then someone could sell my statue on Amazon.

Where was I?

Oh yeah! After Mr. Macadoo left, Pappaw and I talked for a while more until Mom showed up to take me home. But not before Pappaw made a list of a few books he believes will help me in my research about grimoires.

In the car, as Mom hummed along to Taylor Swift singing about her latest breakup, I thought more about what Pappaw had told me about grimoires. They're like spell books, he said. And that got me wondering about *The Lord of the Rings* and *Harry Potter*.

If what I saw last night was a spell book, then the person in the cloak was a witch or a wizard. Besides what they were doing and why, the question now is whether they're good or bad?

Is the person in the cloak a Gandalf or a Saruman?

A Dumbledore or a Voldemort?

Let me know what you think in the comments.

Ep. 7: The Bad Kind

Knighthood Never Looked So Good - 478 Views

The majority of you think we're dealing with a Voldemort/Saruman type of wizard or witch here.

And I think you might be right. Here's why.

After another boring day of school where I sat by myself at lunch, I rode my bike to our town's library with Samwise trotting beside me to see if they had any books from Pappaw's list.

The library has a No Pet policy so when we reached the front door, I placed my bike in the rack and knelt down next to Samwise and explained that they only let service dogs in there.

Samwise seemed to understand as he blinked his big brown eyes then sat down. After commanding him not to go chasing any squirrels or cats or tennis balls, and not to talk to strangers even if they have good dog treats, I told him to start barking if he saw anything suspicious, and I would come running. He nuzzled my hand and I gave him a quick hug and a pat on the head, then went in.

My library is old, probably as old as Twin Valley itself, dimly lit, and smells like books. Which if I'm being honest, isn't a terrible smell. I mean, if I owned a candle company, I wouldn't make a scented candle called "old books" or anything but it's not the worst odor to say hi to my nostrils.

Once inside, I went straight to the librarian on duty and showed her my list. She pointed me in the direction of Aisle 13, telling me the books I was looking for were halfway down on my right.

Though I'm not super superstitious and only regular superstitious, the aisle number wasn't lost on me. Of course, books about magical books would be shelved in Aisle 13. Maybe the Dewey Decimal System should be the Devil Decimal System.

Anyway, I searched for each book. I didn't find them all, but I found some and was about to head back to the checkout counter when I caught wind of a conversation happening on the other side of the bookshelf. I'm not usually one to eavesdrop on other people's conversations, but a word seized my attention like the sweet melody of an ice cream truck on a hot summer's day.

"Hexed?" someone said in a hurried whisper.

Hexed isn't a word I normally would have known, but because I'd spent a lot of my Sunday afternoon researching grimoires online, I was aware of it. I crept down the aisle and gently pushed a few books to the side, creating a gap I could peek through. Two women stood in what I think was the love book section, because the spines all had lovey-dovey titles like *Across All Hearts* and *Forever Your Desire*.

No offense if you're a fan of those kind of books but yuck. I'd rather read a math textbook.

Where was I?

Oh yeah! These two women were about the same height as each other and all I could see of their faces were their bright red lips moving a mile a minute.

I recognized one of the lady's voices. Her name is Meg. Her husband, Phil, is my school's maintenance guy. He's also the town's umpire for little league games. The one year I played, I saw him at every game. His wife was there too. She sat with all the moms talking up a storm and she has a sort of nasally high-pitched voice, so it really stands out in a crowd. I didn't recognize the other lady at all.

Anyway, the other lady was like, "Hexed? I didn't know you believed in the supernatural, Meg."

Meg said she didn't... at least until last night when her husband, Phil, started acting like he was in a zombie movie. That really caught the other lady off guard because she broke the library's most sacred rule when she cried out, "Zombie movie!"

I expected the librarians to come drag her away, but they didn't. Instead, Meg pressed a finger to her lips and quieted the other lady down before whispering about how Phil was stumbling around looking for something and mumbling a bunch of nonsense in a language she didn't understand.

When she said that, I thought about the ratty robe person chanting, and my ears really perked up. I leaned closer.

The other woman smiled in a strange sort of way and made a joke about the "language of love," whatever that was supposed to mean. But Meg didn't find it funny as she went all serious, lowering her voice even more and saying, "I'm telling ya, somethings going on and I think I know—"

That was when somebody coughed from nearby. It was one of the librarians and she was standing in Aisle 13 watching me. She shot me a look of disapproval for eavesdropping, then said I needed to check out my books.

I know what you're thinking: *Right at the good part*.

I followed the librarian to the checkout counter. Just as she scanned the last book, Samwise started barking like mad. And it was that same deep bark from Saturday. I slid the stack of books into my bag and made a mad dash toward the exit.

Samwise was right where I left him but standing tall and stiff. The hair on his back bristled as he growled and barked, his stare fixed right ahead. I followed his gaze until I saw it.

The maroon car! It joined a line of cars waiting for our town's only stoplight to turn from red to green.

I whispered to Samwise that I saw it and he stopped barking. Bending low, I hurried to a nearby oak tree to get a better look and Samwise followed. Just as I got close enough to see the driver, the stoplight turned green, and the cars began moving again.

I drew my lips into a line like this… and peered down at Samwise and told him, "You know what we have to do, don't you?"

Samwise barked his approval, so I rushed over to my bike. And you won't believe what happened next.

But you'll have to wait for my next video for that.

Ep. 8: Gone, baby, Gone

Knighthood Never Looked So Good - 569 Views

I read some of your comments and I agree, ending my previous video like that was kind of a cheap move, but as my pappaw likes to say, "Leave 'em wanting more." And I'm not making you wait *that* long.

Anyway, back to what happened.

I jumped on my bike and headed for the sidewalk. If spy movies have taught me anything, the key to following someone is to stay close but not too close, so that's what Samwise and I tried to do. Dodging a troop of girl scouts and a speedy mailman, we caught up to the maroon car.

I don't know what my goal was exactly, I hadn't really thought it through, but I worked my way closer until the car's brake lights lit up suddenly. I stopped too, my bike tire skidding on the dust at the edge of the sidewalk. Samwise reared back on his hind legs and growled.

A couple seconds passed where the world froze and my entire body clenched up. Did they spot me? And then with a squeal of rubber on asphalt, the maroon car roared to life again. I slammed the soles of my gym shoes onto the pedals and my bike lurched forward.

"Come on, Sam!" I cried. "We can't let them get away."

I pedaled so hard my bones rattled and we gained ground. Samwise was a brown and black blur beside me, his tongue flapping in the breeze.

Up ahead a train of cars formed behind a tractor trundling through town in what I would call perfect timing. My stomach spun. We *were* gonna get them!

But then the car's driver stood on the brakes and the car squealed to a stop. I didn't this time, however, and neither did Samwise. We were going too fast!

Eventually, my front tire smacked against a chunk of broken sidewalk, stopping the momentum of the bike and sending me flyin' over the handlebars. I landed hard on my back in the nearby grass.

Head spinning, I clung to the last bit of breath in my lungs. Samwise scampered over to me and licked my forehead.

It took me a couple of seconds to regain my composure, but it came back real quick when I heard the sound of a car door opening nearby. Samwise snapped to attention, and I rolled over and climbed to my feet.

The driver was getting out but must've changed his mind when he saw me stand up, because he slammed that car door shut again. And I say "he" because I finally saw enough of his stubbly jawline to confirm what I already suspected, but sadly not enough to identify him. It was only a glimpse before the driver climbed back into the car then yanked the steering wheel to the right, accelerating into a nearby alley. But a glimpse is all I needed to know who was behind the wheel, because those glowing white eyes flashed, stopping me cold in my tracks.

Those glowing white eyes may have caught me in a spell for a moment, but fortunately for me, Samwise and I know our town like the bottom of his paw.

"That alley's a dead end!" I said to Samwise. "Let's go!"

I don't know if it was my adrenaline gland or whatever, but we didn't hesitate a second longer before we charged around the corner into the alley. We were ready to get to the bottom of this mystery.

But there was no bottom to get to. The driver and the car had vanished.

I'm not kidding. There was nothing but a couple of trash cans and some broken glass in that alley.

I rubbed my head in disbelief while Samwise sniffed around.

You probably don't believe me, but it happened. That car disappeared and I don't know how. I'm hoping one of these books Pappaw recommended will tell me.

Whatever I discover, I'm pretty sure there's a powerful wizard out there hexing people in my town. And as a Paladin Knight-in-Training, it's my duty to put a stop to him.

Ep. 9: Loser
Knighthood Never Looked So Good - 671 Views

You know what stinks?

When your best friend decides he's too cool to hang out with you anymore.

And that's what happened today—well that wasn't the only thing. I also got sent to the principal's office—but losing my best friend was like the worst thing.

After I posted yesterday's video, I tossed and turned for a long time. The man with the white glowing eyes? His weird chanting by the fire? Meg's husband, Phil, getting hexed? The disappearing car? My heart pounded in my chest and my mind spun as fast as Samwise when he's chasing his stub of a tail when he's got an itch.

I couldn't sort it all out. I had to bounce my ideas off someone other than Samwise. Don't get me wrong. He's as loyal as anyone I know, but I needed someone who wouldn't get caught up in licking his own butt in the middle of our conversation.

What, Sam? It's true and you know it. Butt licking is like your number four hobby behind eating, sleeping, and chasing whatever rodent or cat dares to step into our yard.

Anyway, as I was saying. I needed someone I could trust who wouldn't tell my mom. My immediate thought was Ruth. So I went to her room. Light shone from underneath her door and I could hear her talking so I knew I wouldn't be waking her up. I turned the knob and pushed it open.

I'm not going to describe to you what I saw. All I can say is I'm surprised I'm not blind. I guess I pinched my eyes shut just in time.

But as scarring as it was seeing my sister in her skivvies, what bothered me most was how she was talking to herself in the mirror. Why all of a sudden does she think she's ugly and fat? That isn't even true and who cares when you have as much fun as she does… or used to?

Needless to say, she chased me out before I could even explain myself. And now I'm permanently banned from her room, which is lousy because sometimes, when I have nightmares and get scared, she lets me sleep in her bed with her.

I mean, when I *used* to get scared. I definitely don't anymore… definitely.

Since Ruth was no longer an option, I crept downstairs and nabbed our cordless phone which is connected to our landline. You probably don't have a landline phone—not many people do—but Mom and Dad keep it around for business reasons, I think. I'm glad they do because it's my main source of communication with the outside world besides my laptop.

That's a little bit of a sore subject between me and my parents. Maybe when I'm a Paladin Knight, they'll let me have my own phone.

Hurston has his own phone so calling him didn't risk waking up his parents and getting him in trouble. He didn't answer the first or second time I called. It was the third try when he finally picked up. And when he did, he sounded kind of distracted.

I was like, "Hey Hurston, it's me. There's something really important we need to talk about." And he was like, "Is it about me not calling you over the weekend because we... were umm... doing family stuff and I—"

I cut him off because it obviously wasn't about that. I went on to explain about how me and Samwise went down to the Swafford's old place and we heard this chanting from the woods and eventually we found a wizard with glowing white eyes. However, the entire time he just said, "Ah-huh. Ah-huh, Ah-huh, Ah-huh." So I stopped and the phone went silent for a few seconds, apart from the sounds of button mashing from his end. And then I asked him what he thought about the evil wizard with glowing eyes that chased us out of the woods, and he said, and I quote: "It's cool."

His answer told me he wasn't really listening because the Hurston Flores I know wouldn't have ever said an evil wizard was cool. He's a Paladin Knight-in-Training like me, or at least I think he is...

Well, I still needed his help, so I asked, "Did you even hear what I said? I saw an EVIL wizard!" And he was like, "Yeah, I heard you, but I'm kinda in the middle of something here. Can we talk about it in the morning?" So we agreed to meet up at school the next day. Which was today.

He ended the call and I guess went back to playing video games, probably with the new kid, Levi.

Well, today at school, I tried repeatedly to talk to him, but I couldn't get him alone. I even left him a note stuck in his locker instructing him to meet me after school at our usual place, the picnic shelter at our town's rundown park across from the public pool.

But he didn't show.

I waited for ages, and I would've kept waiting, if a group of older kids who smelled like cigarette smoke hadn't shown up and taken over the place.

As I rode home, I told myself Hurston probably forgot and went home, but that hope was soon dashed when I spotted his bike laying in the grass with a couple of others next to the Corner Cupboard, our town's tiny ice cream shop. He was with Levi and a few other kids from my grade, eating ice cream, and playing on their phones.

He blew me off to hang out with Levi and the worst thing is:

Hurston doesn't even like ice cream. He's lactose intolerant!

Ugh!

I slunk away feeling pretty sure my best friend is too cool to hang out with me.

Which also means I'm solo on this journey to stop an evil wizard.

Well, not completely solo.

I have you, Samwise. Now come here for a hug. I could use one.

Ep. 10: The Principal's Office
Knighthood Never Looked So Good - 671 Views

Based on your comments on my last video, you want to know why I got sent to the principal's office.

It's kind of complicated but here it goes.

There's this girl who sits in front of me in Math class named Usha Patel. She has dark eyes and really long black hair that almost touches the ground when she's sitting in her seat. I don't really know her that well. She moved to our school a year ago or something, but this is the first year we've been in the same classes. We have homeroom and Math together.

She plays tennis. I know that because I've seen her and her dad out practicing at the public tennis courts. When they're practicing, I usually hear her dad yelling before I reach the courts. Also, sometimes she has her racket hooked around her book bag and it swings side to side like a wide dragon's tail when she walks through the school hallway.

Anyway, in Ms. Hefflestine's Math class, we were passing up our homework from the night before when Usha began to freak out. Her eyes went wide with panic and she started scrounging through her stuff like she was a raccoon digging in a trash can.

"Where is it? Where is it? Where is it?" she kept saying.

And then Medusa's sister cleared her throat, peered over the new kid to Usha and was like, "Usha? Your homework?" which only caused Usha to freak out even more. After a few seconds, Ms. Hefflestine began tapping her foot. It was so quiet, each tap sounded like a roll of thunder.

Boom! Boom! Boom!

I'm sure Usha thought that way too because she was in full blown panic mode now with droplets of sweat beading up on her forehead. She swore she had it, saying it was just right there on her desk seconds before. I don't know if it was or not, but Ms. Hefflestine must've forgotten her coffee that morning, because she wasn't having it.

Ms. Hefflestine lifted both eyebrows and said in her snakelike voice, "Well if that *isss* the *cassse,* when you redo your homework, you can turn it in for partial credit."

Usha started to protest before a stern look from Ms. Hefflestine cut her off. Defeated by the threat of statuefication from the harsh gaze of one of Medusa's sisters, Usha sank down into her seat, her face planted into the crook of her elbow, and Ms. Hefflestine moved on with the lesson.

Though I couldn't see Usha's face, I'm pretty sure she was crying. I felt bad for her. I wanted to lean forward and tell her it would be okay and that everyone loses their homework every once in a while—like the one time when Samwise *actually ate* my homework. It was a log cabin made out of candy, so I couldn't really blame him—but I didn't dare speak at all. I couldn't risk the wrath of Ms. Hefflestine coming down on both me and Usha if she caught us talking.

As my mom likes to say, it really was an unfortunate incident. I tried to put it behind me, but later that day in Mr.

Macadoo's Social Studies class, his phone rang, interrupting his lively retelling of the Boston Massacre. And I mean *lively*. He painted such a vivid picture; it was like he was there when it happened or something.

Anyway, Mr. Macadoo's phone rang, and he hurried to his desk to answer it. After a short conversation, he hung up and turned to me.

"Paul, grab your things," he said, all serious like. "Mr. Brindle wants to see you in his office."

As soon as he said my name it felt like all the spy satellites and telescopes in space with their super enhanced cameras turned their attention on me.

I can't be certain of that, but I know for sure all the eyes of my classmates found me.

I froze.

Getting called to the office is a big deal. Getting called to the principal's office is an even bigger deal.

Mr. Brindle is kind of scary. He's a large man with a crew cut who always wears a black bow tie and white dress shirt. The older kids on the bus used to call him the Hawk because he has a beak-like nose and thick glasses that make his eyes bulge out of their sockets.

"Be careful at the Middle school," they used to say, "or the Hawk will swoop down and get you!"

And to make things worse, he never smiles. At least, not a single student in the history of Twin Valley Middle School has seen him smile. You can ask around if you don't believe me.

I asked my mom once if she remembered seeing Mr. Brindle smile when she went to the Middle School and she laughed at the question. "I don't think the man can smile," I remember her saying. "I think his face is made of marble."

So, in the aftermath of Mr. Brindle's request to see me, I couldn't move. All I could do was watch the shadow of a hawk circling my desk. But Mr. Macadoo broke me out of it.

Mr. Macadoo peered at me the way my pappaw does when he's trying to make me feel better about something, then said, "Don't worry, you'll be fine."

And that's what it took to get me moving, though I still felt like I was a death row inmate heading to the electric chair.

Mr. Brindle's door was open when I reached the office. I stopped short of it, but the Hawk still saw me.

"Mr. Weaver," he squawked, sounding more birdlike than any human should. "Place your things on my desk and have a seat."

I swallowed hard and stepped into his nest—I mean—office, which if I'm being honest, left a lot to be desired with its mostly bare walls, cobwebbed corners, and thin lime green carpet. Peering down from atop a tall filing cabinet, coiled up and waiting to pounce, a wood carved panther—our school's mascot—was the only thing that added any personality to the room.

Mr. Brindle carved it himself, some say, from the wood of the original cabin that was our town's first schoolhouse. Or from the casket of one of his first victims.

Mr. Brindle sat at his desk, his thick glasses perched at the end of his beak—I mean—nose, reading over a piece of paper, making me stew for a little while.

I'm not going to lie. Being in his office turned my insides into melted butter.

Until finally, he was like, "Mr. Weaver, you know stealing is wrong, don't you?" And I was like, "Yes sir, I do." Which I may not have said out loud because words were hard to come by at that moment. But I definitely nodded and he followed with, "And you know stealing someone else's homework is considered cheating?"

I hesitated for a second because my brain was making a connection to something that caused my knee to bounce up and down like it does when I get nervous. So he repeated the question and I pushed down my knee to keep it from bouncing and managed a "Yes. Why are you asking me this?"

And he was like, "Well, Ms. Patel's math homework went missing."

And I felt the injustice of his inferred accusation like a sudden blast of heat. Leaping to my feet, I yelled, "That doesn't mean I stole it! I demand to see my lawyer!"

Okay. I didn't do that.

I just bit down on my lip long enough for me to figure out how to deny I had anything to do with it—which is true—while pointing out how stealing is against the Paladin Knight's Code of Honor.

Unless it is in pursuit of justice.

I don't think stealing homework meets that criterion though. And something told me Mr. Brindle wouldn't accept that argument anyway because the next thing he did was look up from the paper in his hands with those bulging eyes and say, "I'd like to believe you didn't take it, but I have a letter written by one of your classmates telling me he saw you grab Ms. Patel's math homework from her desk as some kind of prank."

I'd been set up!

I denied stealing the homework of course, pointing out that I barely even know Usha. And of course, the Hawk wasn't buying it. He arched an eyebrow and said, "So you wouldn't mind if I looked through some of your things?"

I didn't know what to say, so I just shoved my pile of stuff across the desk at him. He pushed the glasses up on his nose and began rummaging through it.

He flipped through each folder, dumped out the contents of my lunch box and then my pencil pouch. He poked through it, before mixing everything up into one big pile and brushing it all back into my pencil pouch. He even pinched my textbooks by their covers and shook 'em out like he was looking for a quarter in a pair of jeans. When he was satisfied, he pushed the stack back toward me.

I crossed my arms, feeling the thrill of vindication, which is a big word my parents like to use that means being right.

But to my dismay, his search was not yet concluded. Because he rose to his feet and, placing his hands on his hips like this... demanded I take him to my locker.

So that's what I did and the entire walk from his office to my locker, I kept my back as straight as possible. I didn't want him to know I was afraid. I mean, I didn't want him to even think I was afraid, though I totally wasn't.

The next thing that happened was the most nerve-racking experience of my life.

I had to open the locker with him standing over me. I bet some of you can relate to the daily challenge of mastering a combination lock. I'm not so great with mine on a normal day as sometimes I get the numbers all jumbled up, but add the pressure of a bird man with a stern Roman statue of a scowl looming over me... and I didn't stand much of a chance.

It took several tries with my sweaty hands and trembling fingers before I finally got it. And when I did, Mr. Brindle almost knocked me down to continue his pursuit. You would've thought he was searching for his debit card or *the ring of power* from the way he dug through my things.

He eventually got to my book bag, unzipped it, pulled out each individual book and shook them like he had in his office, then sat them in a stack on the floor.

Like I told him, I didn't steal the homework, so his search turned up nothing.

When he was finished, he grumbled under his breath and stepped back, rubbing his forehead. Then his gaze narrowed on the pile of items he'd pulled from my bag. He snatched the top book off the stack and read the title aloud, "*Grimoires and Other Mysterious Books*." Then he tilted his eyebrows above his glasses and asked me why I was reading it.

I couldn't tell him the full truth, so I told him the half-truth. That my pappaw had recommended it to me.

But Mr. Brindle didn't buy that. He stared at me with those bulging eyes and was like, "Your grandfather recommended this to you?" I pointed out my pappaw was a history doctor who liked old books and Mr. Brindle just rubbed his chin with his free hand, and said, "Is that so?"

Then he gestured for me to go back to class, and I hurried to shove everything back in my locker. I was about to shut it when Mr. Brindle cleared his throat.

Suddenly filled with a sense of dread that made my stomach melted butter again, I turned around. The Hawk loomed over me.

"You forgot this one," he said, extending the book he'd taken off the top of the stack.

I reached for it, but he didn't let me have it right away.

Instead, he held onto it and said something I still can't wrap my head around: "Sometimes people steal from others for what they think is the right reason, but almost every time, they bite off more than they can chew."

I thought at the time it had something to do with Usha's homework, though I'm not so sure now... but anyway, I respectfully reminded him I didn't steal Usha's homework. And all he said was that he hoped that was true before letting me take the book from his hands.

He didn't add "or else" but he didn't have to. I gulped, slid the book into my bag and shut my locker.

I didn't say anything else after that and neither did he. We went our separate ways, he to his nest and me to Mr. Macadoo's class.

And that's why I got sent to the principal's office. Not that exciting really and definitely not worse than my best friend standing me up—

Wait.

What if Hurston didn't stand me up?

What if he never knew he was even supposed to meet me?

Hmmm...

Mr. Brindle said someone gave him a note saying I stole Usha's homework. He referred to that someone as a "he."

This might sound crazy at first, but hear me out.

What if someone set me up in hopes that the Hawk would give me a detention so Hurston and I couldn't meet?

But when that didn't happen, this someone resorted to swiping the note from Hurston's locker.

This someone would've had to see me write the note to Hurston *and* been close enough to Usha to steal her homework *and* been close enough to Hurston to steal the note from his locker, then blame it on me. And this someone would have to be a boy who wanted Hurston all to himself.

And if you haven't guessed it yet, I have the perfect suspect in mind. Someone with motive and opportunity.

The new kid, Levi.

He's trying to steal my best friend.

I can't let that happen.

Ep. 11: The Fight
Knighthood Never Looked So Good - 1,379 Views

Have any of you ever been in a fight at school?

What did you feel like afterward?

After your heart stopped racing and the anger went away, did you feel... kind of hollow inside?

I've never been in a fight before and I'm not sure what happened today even qualified as one, though the other kids at school kept calling it a fight.

You can decide for yourself after I tell you what happened, but know when I got to school, I didn't intend for what happened to happen.

That's a lot of happening.

Anyway, when I walked into school today, I got a weird feeling, like everyone was watching me and not in a good way. It was like my skin crawled, for real. Everyone kept giving me side-eye glances then turned away like I had the plague or something. Then in the lunch line, I heard a kid from Levi and Hurston's table whispering in front of me.

He was like, "Be careful. Paul's behind us. He'll pocket your lunch money."

That's when it all clicked into place. Levi hadn't just written an anonymous letter to Mr. Brindle, he told the whole school I stole Usha's homework! Of course, I couldn't let that stand.

"I didn't steal anything!" I told the kid. "Levi's lying!" And the kid whipped around and was like, "Not only are you a thief, but now you spy on other people's conversations?"

I pointed out he said my name which gives me the right to listen, and he fired back with, "You probably think you had *the right* to steal Usha's homework, don't you?"

I clenched my fists I was so mad, and insisted I *didn't* steal Usha's homework. But the kid just shrugged and walked away with his tray of lunch food as if it was no big deal that the entire school believes I'm a thief.

But it *is* a big deal because those kinds of accusations *stick*. I don't know how things work at your school but at my school, you're guilty until proven innocent and rumors are written in wet cement.

So I ate my lunch alone—again—a thousand percent certain that every table's conversations were about me. And the entire time, Hurston and Levi were huddled together across the lunchroom cracking up at something.

I'm not going to lie, my blood boiled. Hurston should've been over here at our table, cracking jokes with me or helping me plan our next move to track down this wizard, or mapping out the next part of our town we wanted to explore, or brainstorming video ideas, or making fun of the sisters of Medusa—not over there worrying about some Snapchat streak or whatever.

It was hard to focus in class the rest of the day and not for my normal reasons, but because people kept making snide comments or whispering things about me. During Science class someone hit me on the back of the head with a crumpled piece of paper which had the word thief written like 500 times on it. Each with an exclamation point.

My body heated up like I was a cartoon character who ate a super spicy pepper. There might've been steam shooting out of my ears—I don't know—but I stood up, turned around, and said, "I'm a Paladin Knight-in-Training not a common thief!"

And then my teacher, Mrs. Plotter, made things worse. She looked up from the magazine she was reading at her desk and was like, "Mr. Weaver, I don't care what you are. Sit down and be quiet!"

And then everyone laughed. So when that class ended, I went to recess feeling both angry and embarrassed… angbarrassed or is it emgry?

I'm going with angbarrassed.

I went to recess feeling angbarrassed, and an angbarrassed person is like a stick of TNT with a short fuse.

So, I wasn't exactly in a great state of mind when one of Usha's friends stomped over to me and was like, "Do you know what you've done, Paul? Usha's dad is so mad at her that he took her phone away and she can't come to my birthday party this weekend! She's over there crying."

I told her I didn't take that stupid assignment and she pointed a finger in my face and said, "Yes you did! Levi saw you in Brindle's office being questioned about it."

Then I said something that, now that I think about it, probably made things worse. I said, "That doesn't mean I took it, you dummy."

I know. I shouldn't have called her a dummy, but I was mad

and she wasn't being logical.

It didn't matter what I said, though, because she ignored my comment and added, "All because you have a crush on Usha and you don't know how to be normal around girls! Or normal at all!"

Crush on Usha?

Crush on Usha!

Apparently, Levi was telling everyone that.

Now I was *really* mad. I squeezed my fists and clenched my teeth. If Usha's friend said something else, I didn't hear it. Like Sauron's evil eye, my gaze shifted across the playground to Levi, who stood with Hurston and a handful of other people, spinning a basketball on his finger.

My surging angbarrassment taking over, I brushed past Usha's friend, tromped over to Levi, and smacked the ball right off his fingertip.

Levi's jaw dropped and he was like, "What the heck, Paul?"

And I was like, "Wha—What the heck to you. You think you can just move here and start rumors about people?" And he just scrunched his face and said, "I don't know what you're talking about."

I told him not to play dumb and that I knew what he did and why he did it. And he looked around in the air as if he was clueless before settling his gaze on Hurston who just shrugged. Which made me even madder for some reason.

So I was like, "Let me clear things up for you. You wrote a letter to Mr. Brindle saying I was the one who took Usha's homework, trying to get me in trouble!"

And he just sneered as if the mere idea was impossible. Well, I've got news for you, Levi. I don't even know what "mere" means!

Anyway, I nodded toward Hurston and said, "Because you didn't want Hurston to hang out with me after school. And when I didn't get a detention like you hoped, you just took the note I wrote for Hurston from his locker!"

And what he did next *really* sent me over the edge.

Laughing and shaking his head, he was like, "Paul, I guess what everyone says about you is true. You really are crazy!"

And when he said that, I saw red! I even let out a growl! Then I pushed him with both hands as hard as I could. He stumbled back and fell into one of his friends. Then I saw his eyes flash and he came back at me.

Even though Levi's bigger than me, I stood my ground. I wasn't afraid. But before he could get to me, Hurston jumped between us, urging us to stop.

We did, but my heart was pounding, and I felt like Samwise when his hair stands up on the back of his neck. And then the arguing began.

"He started it!" Levi said, and I was like, "No, I didn't. You tried to steal my best friend!"

And he was like, "No, I didn't."

And I said, "Yes you did!"

By that point all the kids at recess had surrounded us like a jury weighing the evidence.

So I pointed at Levi and was like, "He's lying. He's—"

And that's when Hurston cut me off and told me the truth: Levi wasn't lying. When I asked him how he knew that, he went quiet for a moment, glanced down at the ground, and confessed that he saw my note.

I couldn't believe it. I… I couldn't.

"What?" I stammered out. "You did?" And he looked back up

at me and said, "I didn't meet you there because... because I'm done with that stuff."

I shook my head, refusing to accept it. I tried explaining that what I wrote in that note wasn't just *stuff*. That it's all true. There's an evil wizard hexing our town, but...

But he was like, "For real, Paul? Evil wizards and magic books? I'm over it."

"How can you be over it?" I said and reminded him that we're Paladin Knights-in-Training and that we have a channel.

He stopped me there and said, "No. You have a channel. And I don't even subscribe anymore."

I went to argue my case, but Hurston wouldn't hear it. He said, flatly, "Look Paul. We're not little kids anymore." Then he added, "At least I'm not."

I'm not going to lie. That cut me deep.

And that's when Mr. Macadoo came over and everybody kind of just scattered, leaving me alone.

So, was it a fight?

I don't know.

All I know is when the dust settled, I felt like I'd lost.

Because I have.

My first subscriber. But more importantly, my best friend.

Ep. 12: 73.6%

Knighthood Never Looked So Good - 1,512 Views

I had a conversation with Mr. Macadoo today that made me do a lot of thinking and led me somewhere that I think will surprise you.

At the end of Social Studies, right when we were dismissed for lunch, I was packing up my things when Mr. Macadoo said he would like to chat for a few minutes.

I slowly sank down into my chair, certain I was in some kind of trouble, but he put me at ease right away when he said, "Don't worry, Paul, you're not in trouble. I just want to make sure you're okay."

I didn't say anything because... well, I didn't know what to say.

Mr. Macadoo sat down on top of the desk and placed one of his legs in the chair and said that after gathering intel about my little scuffle from the day before, he'd come to learn there's rumors going around about me that he didn't particularly like. Before I could even dispute them, he assured me he didn't believe a word of those rumors and said, "Just because a teacher or a principal questions a student about something, it doesn't mean that student is guilty."

Before you say it, *I know*! Finally, someone is being logical.

He also said that doesn't mean he approves of me fighting people over the rumors, which I understand. He did clarify that he knew where I was coming from because he's had people say awful things about him too.

Which I found hard to believe considering he's probably the nicest teacher I've ever had.

But he swore that was the case and was like, "People have said some truly awful things about me, mostly out of ignorance, but yes, I've been in your shoes."

I couldn't picture him fighting anyone, but I still had to ask, so I was like, "When they did that, what did you do?" And he paused for a moment, then reached up and rubbed something under the collar of his shirt—or whatever is attached to his gold necklace and said something really deep. He said, "I lived my life as true to myself as possible. As corny as it may sound, letting love guide me. And if needed, I forgave them."

Okay. He was right, it was corny. But also deep.

Anyway, I asked him why he forgave them and he told me that carrying around a lot of anger doesn't do anyone any good. Me or the other person. He then encouraged me to go to lunch and give what he said some thought.

So that's what I did and for a little while I forgot all about the evil wizard who may be hexing people in my town.

I thought first about Levi and Hurston and then I thought about another person lost in all of this...

Usha.

She hadn't wronged me and I hadn't wronged her, but the

image of her crying at school and stuff made me feel guilty inside. So, I decided I would speak with her, to make things right.

I couldn't risk talking to her at school because, you know, the whole crush rumor—which is a million times infinity untrue—so Samwise and I made a trip to the one place I was certain to find her away from the prying eyes of our classmates.

I was right. We found Usha practicing at Twin Valley's public tennis courts. I didn't see her dad anywhere. Usha was serving ball after ball into a series of baskets spread out on the opposite side of the court.

My mouth literally fell open and my eyes boggled.

Usha had skill.

She was Legolas from *The Lord of the Rings,* but with a tennis racket.

After she finished that round, I stepped onto the court, cleared my throat, and awkwardly offered to help her get the tennis balls out of the baskets.

She was skeptical of course. Her eyes narrowed, and she was like, "What are you doing here?" And I was like, "I didn't come to steal anything from you. Just like I didn't steal your homework. I only want to talk." I even held up my hands and showed her my palms like this...

She hesitated for a few seconds but agreed to let me help.

I nodded and walked around the net to the opposite court. Samwise came with me. I picked up one of the baskets and told her that although I definitely didn't steal her homework, I was sorry that it happened.

When she asked me why I was sorry if I wasn't the person who stole her homework, I dumped the balls into a bucket by the net, shrugged, and answered, "I don't know exactly. I saw you crying at school and now you're grounded and... it makes me feel bad for you."

When I said that, she was like, "You don't have to feel bad. I'll be fine."

She may've said she'd be fine, but the way she slumped her shoulders and drug her feet said otherwise. It was the opposite of how she looked just minutes before when she was the Legolas of the tennis court.

I told her I wish it hadn't happened. And that, she agreed with. Then she said something that made me feel real bad for her.

She picked up one of the tennis balls, bounced it a couple times, and was like, "I knew my dad would be mad when he saw a zero in the online gradebook. But I didn't expect him to get as mad as he got. He took my phone and grounded me from pretty much everything but tennis."

That's a lot for only one bad grade and I told her that. She agreed with me on that, too, informing me that her dad's been extra grouchy lately.

I've seen Mr. Patel at the courts. He's... what's that word for loud and intense? It starts with an 'A'...

Aggressive!

Like I was saying, Mr. Patel is aggressive when he's coaching her. It's kind of scary. That's probably why she cried so much.

By that point there were only a couple baskets remaining. I grabbed one, then asked her if she maybe accidentally threw her homework away. But she swore it was on her desk and then it just vanished.

I asked her if she checked just in case, and she smirked at me and was like, "Now you sound like my step-mother. But yes.

I checked every trash can, even the one under the teacher's desk."

I stopped suddenly, because that was impressive. One doesn't dare venture into the domain of a sister of Medusa. That took some real courage.

When I told her that, Usha actually broke a smile which kicked up butterflies in my stomach for some reason.

Usha couldn't believe I referred to Ms. Hefflestine as a sister of a hideous monster from Greek mythology, and argued that she wasn't that bad.

"Yes, she is," I argued back. "She probably keeps a collection of students she turned into statues in her garden like the lady from *Percy Jackson*."

To drive my point home, I dropped the basket and pretended to slowly turn to stone making sound effects and everything. And Usha actually laughed. Like for real. Which made me feel kind of warm inside.

Don't read too much into that. I was happy to see she wasn't so sad and angry anymore. That's all.

Really.

Anyway, Usha laughed and said, "You're right, she is that bad," and I was like, "No kidding! And you actually ventured into her domain!"

And that's when she told me she discovered something strange. She said she found a charred piece of paper with a love poem on it.

"A what?" I asked, because that's a totally weird thing to find under a sister of Medusa's desk.

Usha said it was a piece of paper, burned up mostly, with

lyrics from a love poem on it. Something about a soul reaver. She wasn't sure.

I told her that was strange, and she agreed saying, "I didn't take Ms. Hefflestine for the romantic type, but maybe there's a Mr. Medusa out there."

I shrugged and said, "Maybe," choosing to keep my real, not so optimistic, thoughts to myself. But Usha, she seemed to like the possibility. She poured another basket of tennis balls into the bucket, then stared off into the distance and whispered, "I hope there is."

And she really seemed to mean it.

And that's when Samwise, attempting to get a ball out of the last basket, flipped the basket over on himself, spilling the balls across the court, and getting himself trapped in the process. Usha laughed and I said, "Don't mind him, he identifies as a turtle." Which made Usha laugh again.

But her laughter ended when a car's horn blasted, and we both turned to see a red truck pulling into the parking lot.

Usha frowned and told me it was her dad, that me and Samwise better go. Because Mr. Patel doesn't like her to have any distractions when she's practicing. But I was actually having fun and wanted to stay a little longer, so I said, "Are you sure? My turtle over there loves to fetch tennis balls. He'd probably be pretty helpful."

Usha smiled, but this time it looked tinged with worry. She didn't say yes she was sure, but she didn't have to. I understood, so I whistled for Samwise, who crawled out of his shell, his head hanging with disappointment.

But then, when I climbed on my bike and started to peddle away, Usha called out to me. I stopped and she was like, "Thanks for... ummm... helping me clean up. And for the record, I'm approximately 73.6% sure you didn't take my homework."

I smiled and told her I was hoping for 73.7%, but I'd take it.

She laughed again as me and my corgi turtle rode away.

So, as you can see, not a lot happened today.

Ep. 13: Oh no!

Knighthood Never Looked So Good - 1,512 Views

Something happened to Pappaw.

If you're wondering, that's why I look so pale.

When I got to school today, no one was talking about Usha and me which meant no one saw us at the tennis court. Phew. But I still felt weird about how everything went down with Hurston and Levi.

Mr. Macadoo said I should forgive them but... I don't know. It still hurts. Plus, what Hurston said about us not being little kids anymore really sticks in my craw, as my pappaw likes to say.

FYI, a craw is your throat, so what Hurston said hasn't went down easy, like when I'm eating a bag of Doritos real fast and one of them gets stuck in the back of my mouth.

I know we're not little kids anymore, but that doesn't mean we have to change everything about who we are, right? We don't have to suddenly stop wanting to explore our town, stop watching cartoons, and stop reading comic books, right?

Right?

That question is what led me to decide to see Pappaw after school. Because if anyone knows if it is time for me to stop watching cartoons and reading comic books, it would be him. I also hoped for some guidance about how to find the evil wizard.

Ruth—who was still refusing to talk to me since I walked in on her talking to herself in the mirror—was home when I got back from school. Though I apologized for walking in on her, it took Dad calling her on her phone before she eventually agreed to take me to see Pappaw.

With Samwise riding on my lap, watching the scenery pass by with his big bright eyes, we drove to Pappaw's nursing home. Ruth pulled the car to a stop near the entrance. I asked if she wanted to join us and she broke her punitive vow of silence long enough to say, "I can't do it. I just can't see him that way."

I should've seen her comment as a warning, but I didn't know what she meant—at least not then.

Anyway, Ruth promised to be back in an hour then pulled away. Samwise and I passed through the main entrance.

An old woman who looked a lot like Betty White sat in an armchair crocheting or knitting something, her walker sitting beside her like Samwise sits beside me. Her sweater had a kitten on it. She smiled as I walked by and was like, "I like that corgi." I smiled back and said, "Thanks. I like that kitten."

And I did. I know dogs and cats are supposed to be natural born enemies stuck in some kind of eternal blood feud, but I really don't get it. A person can like both.

Speaking of natural born enemies. At that moment, one approached from Pappaw's hallway. It was Mr. Brindle—A.K.A. the Hawk—A.K.A. my principal—walking with purpose right toward me.

I froze in terror.

If you thought running into your teacher in public was awkward, running into your principal—especially one who thinks you're a thief—is about a million times worse.

The old lady must've sensed my principal-induced terror as she nodded and whispered, "Over here, I'll hide ya."

Thawing just in time, I hurried over with Samwise right behind me. We pressed ourselves against the wall next to her chair. The old woman shifted in her seat and pretending to admire her crocheting or knitting or whatever she was crafting, she held it up, shielding us from Mr. Brindle's view.

I didn't exhale until the glass doors slid shut behind him.

I told her thanks, and she asked if Mr. Brindle was one of my teachers and I was like, "Worse. He's my principal." Then I made a cringe face like this... and the old lady chuckled.

After that she got this longing look in her eye, like our conversation reminded her of something from a long time ago, and was like, "Oh, what I would do to be young again."

I was tempted to ask her what she was thinking about. I didn't, however, because my real mission was visiting Pappaw. But then she got kind of serious like she was going to scold me and added, "Enjoy your youth before it's taken from you."

I don't really know what she meant by that, but I told her I would try and then Samwise and I ventured on while she went back to her work.

I waved to the nurse at the front desk and walked to Pappaw's room where I stopped at his open door.

"Okay," I said, turning to Samwise, "I promised Pappaw I would bring you along next time, so we're gonna surprise him." I instructed Samwise to wait until I whistled for him, then run in and really let him have it. And the good little hobbit dog Samwise is, he did just that, taking a seat just outside the doorway, his stub of a tail fluttering side to side.

Knocking on the doorframe, I stepped into the room and called for Pappaw.

The light was off, and the curtains pulled shut. Pappaw lay on his back, his head turned away from the door. He was mumbling something.

I'm not sure why, but at that moment, goosebumps bubbled up all over my arms.

I waited for a few seconds then said louder, "Pappaw. Pappaw!" Which startled him, because he turned around all wide-eyed and snapped, "Who is it? Who is it?"

"It's me, Paul," I told him, reaching for the light switch. "You look like you're having trouble seeing, you want me to turn on the light?"

And he was like, "No! They'll see us. It's safer in the dark."

So I slowly lowered my hand away from the light switch and Pappaw turned his head away from me and began mumbling again.

I took a step closer so I could hear better and my toe touched something on the floor. I bent down to see what it was and my heart sank a little. It was the picture of him and Mammaw. The glass in the frame was splintered. His picture must've fallen off the nightstand next to his bed. But when I asked him about it, he whipped his head back toward me and said, "What picture?"

And I was like, "The one of you and Mammaw?"

His eyes narrowed, then he shook his head and turned away again.

I gently placed the picture back on the nightstand and stood in the silence which was so thick I could have cut it with my Paladin sword. Everything between me and Pappaw always flows so naturally because we are peas and pod according to him. But as I stood silent in the dark, it sure didn't feel that way.

Finally, I decided maybe seeing Samwise would clear things up, so I said, "I brought a surprise for you," and whistled for Samwise.

Just as he'd been told, Samwise came running in, his paws clacking against the tile. He hurried to Pappaw and leaped right into his bed, but Pappaw let out a howl and shoved him off. Samwise fell to the floor with a thud, then scrambled to my side as confused as I was.

Sorry. You will have to give me a second. This next part...

This next part makes me real sad.

And pardon the language.

Well, after Pappaw shoved Samwise out of his bed, he looked at me with utter shock and said, "Why the hell would you bring a dog here?"

I reminded him that last time I was there, he asked me to, but he didn't believe me.

Instead, he shook his head for a moment then, clutching his bed sheets with white knuckles, pulled them close to his face and cried, "Get out of here, the both of you, before you get me killed!"

I hesitated, unsure of what was happening.

But he…

He just repeated it.

"Go!" Pappaw demanded. "Get out of here! Get out of here!"

So that's what I did. Bending down and grabbing Samwise, I sprinted out of the room, down the hall and to the front entrance. I sat on a wooden bench outside, holding Samwise against me, crying into his fur.

You may think I'm a sissy or something for crying like that, but you didn't see Pappaw's eyes. The anger. The fear.

That wasn't my pappaw at all. Or if it was, it was only part of him.

My eyes were all out of tears when Ruth finally got there. When I climbed into the car, I noticed she'd maybe been crying too as her not-Halloween makeup was smudgy on her face. Neither of us felt like talking, so we didn't.

That brings us here. And I keep thinking about how the people I'm closest to have all suddenly changed, you know?

Ruth, Hurston, and now Pappaw. They've changed and not for the better.

Like all of the good and fun stuff about them left.

It's like someone took it—

Wait a sec!

Before I put this on video, I better write it all out and see if it makes sense.

Sorry, guys. That means you'll have to wait.

Ep. 14: You won't believe this!
Knighthood Never Looked So Good - 1,732 Views

I'm not recording this in my room, so yes that's a park behind me and this is a picnic table I'm sitting at.

But anyway. So you know how I was recording yesterday's video and I was hit with an idea?

Well, to make sure it all made sense, I wrote it all out, thought it over a few times, and slept on it.

And guess what? It still makes sense.

You remember how I overheard that lady named Meg in the library talking about how her husband, Phil—our school's maintenance man—was hexed?

What if Phil isn't the only one?

What if the same wizard who hexed him, also hexed Ruth, Hurston, and Pappaw?

It's possible. And I have a theory how. That's why I'm here at the park.

Bark! Bark! Bark!

Don't worry, that's Samwise's excited bark. We're waiting for someone and that someone is here earlier than I expected.

Bark! Bark!

Go ahead, Samwise. Go say hi!

Bark. Bark! Bark...

Hi Usha, I hope Samwise didn't bother you too much. He gets a little excited sometimes.

He's fine... So are you here to apologize again for not stealing my homework?

Depends. Will it make you 73.7% sure it wasn't me?

Ha. Ha. Probably not.

Then no, I'm not here to apologize again for *not* stealing your homework.

Then why are you here?

There's something I have to ask you about. It's on my laptop

Okay?

Remember how you were looking for your homework and you found that love poem written on charred paper in the trash can under Ms. Hefflestine's desk?

You mean sister of Medusa?

Ha. Ha. Right. Well, I might've found it. Take a look.

Okay—Wait, are you recording a video?

Yeah. You got here earlier than I expected, and I was in the middle of one. It's for my channel—no one from school subscribes—but I can turn it off if you want?

Umm... how do I look?

You look pretty—I mean you look fine.

Ummm... okay. I guess I can be in your video.

Cool. Come on over.

Hey everyone. This is Usha.

Ummm. Hi... Now, Paul, what did you want to show me?

Give me a sec and I'll pull it up for you.

Paul, this isn't a prank, right? Like you're going to get me with a jump scare video?

No way! Hurston got me with one once and I nearly peed—never mind. The point is I would never do that to anyone. What I have here is something different. Check it out.

Okay.

That's the love poem I found in Ms. Hefflestine's trash.

Yep, but it's not a poem.

What is it then, a song?

Nope. Usha, do you know what a grimoire is?

A grim-what?

I'll take that as a no. Anyway, a grimoire is a kind of magic book.

Like Harry Potter?

Yes! And that love poem isn't a love poem at all but a spell—

What? You don't believe me?

I don't believe in magical spell books and even if I did, the words don't match.

But they're close, right?

Yeah. But the paper I read started with "Replace the old with the new, the human string, stitch, and glue. Power, beauty, life renewed," or something like that before it went on about a soul reaver.

Okay, but this is close.

Yeah. I said that already.

Then I'm right.

Paul, you're kidding right? You don't really think I found a spell from a magic book?

Ummm… Yes… I mean maybe. I mean—I have a theory.

Let me guess. You think Ms. Hefflestine is trying to cast a love spell.

Not a love spell. A *soul reaver* spell. And I'm not sure it's Ms. Hefflestine.

What's a soul reaver?

According to this website, a soul reaver spell allows a wizard to take part of someone else's soul and merge it with their own.

What?

Yeah. That what it says. Look.

"A dangerous and costly incantation, the soul reaver spell when invoked allows the enchanter to shred a piece of another's soul and temporarily place it in an object before

eventually melding it to their own. The purposes are varied, ranging from mind control to healing from trauma, but most uses have dark intentions. The exact words used in this incantation are unknown and the above is the translation of a portion of the spell found in William Oxford's History of Grimoires. *The authors on this website are in agreement that, even if we had the exact words, it would be our moral responsibility to keep them out of the public eye."*

You actually believe that, Paul?

Yes. I believe everything I read on the internet, don't you?

I'm being serious.

So am I. I mean, not about the believing everything I read on the internet but about my theory.

I don't know...

Look, Usha. I know this all sounds crazy but there's something going on in our town. I've seen some stuff and...

You've seen some stuff?

Yeah.

Like what?

_{A man with glowing eyes driving a vanishing car.}

A what? I couldn't hear you.

A man with glowing eyes driving a vanishing car.

You saw a man with glowing eyes? I thought you said Ms. Hefflestine was behind this?

I don't know, it could've been her. I could be wrong about the man part, but the eyes were definitely glowing.

And this person with glowing eyes is going around stealing pieces of people's souls while driving a vanishing car? Sounds a little out there, doesn't it?

I don't think so.

I… I don't think I agree with you.

Do you believe we have souls?

Yeah, I guess.

Me too.

That doesn't mean someone can steal a piece of it.

I know… but let me read a little more to you and see what you think.

Okay.

"A question arises as to how to tell if you or a loved one has been hexed with a soul reaver spell. On that front we can't give definitive answers, though Dr. Oxford's History of Grimoires seems to suggest that most people who had loved ones believed to have been hexed with the soul reaver spell noticed an abrupt change in personality and behavior—"

Read that last bit again, Paul.

"…most people who had loved ones believed to have been hexed with the soul reaver spell noticed an abrupt change in personality and behavior…"

Hmmm…

Have you noticed an abrupt change in anyone?

Yeah, but that…

But that what?

Never mind.

You can tell me, Usha. Really. I've also noticed an abrupt change—

There's nothing to tell you. Look, Paul, this is all too much, you know? Too much!

But we can—

> *And I gotta get to practice anyway.*

But—

> *I'll talk to you sometime. Bye, Samwise.*

> *Bark!*

Well, I don't think I convinced Usha about my theory. But at least she confirmed my suspicion about what she found in Ms. Hefflestine's trash can. There's still questions though, questions I will have to get answers to because...

Because of what I didn't read to Usha from that website.

The change in personality and behavior is just the beginning.

Or as the website puts it: "*...most people who had loved ones believed to have been hexed with the soul reaver spell noticed an abrupt change in personality and behavior BEFORE a gradual decline in overall health leading to the victim's eventual death.*"

That's right. If this website is accurate and my theory is correct, Ruth, Pappaw, and Hurston could all be in serious danger.

Ep. 15: Plan A or Plan B?
Knighthood Never Looked So Good - 1,805 Views

Hello everyone. I've read your comments and you're right. I need to start with Ms. Hefflestine. She doesn't strike me as the sorceress type, but if reading fantasy novels has taught me anything, it's "don't judge a book by its cover."

Was that a pun?

Maybe?

If so. It was intended.

All right, let's get back to the topic at hand, or paw, if you're Samwise. Since many of you suggested it, I've come up with a plan to investigate Ms. Hefflestine. Well, two plans really. "Plan A" and "Plan B" A.K.A. the risky backup plan I hope I don't have to use.

Let's talk about Plan A first.

Ms. Hefflestine is a sister of Medusa, but with more wrinkles and poofy orange-blonde hair. She doesn't have Principal Brindle's hawkish senses but she's notoriously vicious. If she were to catch me in her room without permission, she'd scream my head off in front of the entire class then have me put in detention for a week. So I need to search her classroom when she's not there. That means the best time is probably lunch. So Plan A is simple: Skip lunch and see what I can find in her room. Because our teachers insist on lining us up to lunch like we're still kindergartners, getting away will be kind of tricky, but it's definitely doable.

Now Plan B?

It'll work, but it's risky and involves me getting myself in trouble and also sneaking contraband into school, which is a cool word meaning stuff you're not supposed to have at school.

Let's hope I don't have to use Plan B.

I'll let you know how I do next time.

Ep. 16: It happened!
Knighthood Never Looked So Good - 2,011 Views

Holy Chocolate Cow!!!!

I have so much to tell you!

My heart is pounding. Feel it.

Never mind, obviously you can't do that. But take my word for it, my heart feels like it might leap out of my chest.

On second thought, that would be a medical emergency. That wouldn't be good because I'm too young to get a Life Alert bracelet.

Yes. I asked.

Anyway, I just got home from school and you guys made the right call to investigate Ms. Hefflestine's room first, though it didn't go as you or I expected it would.

All I can say is we are definitely dealing with a wizard here. A powerful one at that!

Bark! Bark!

Samwise agrees, though he wasn't there. Or maybe he's

hungry. Hold on a sec.

There you go, boy. Snack on that. But don't tell Mom.

All right, back to what happened. So, sneaking away from my class on the way to lunch wasn't so difficult. All it took was a timely shoelace coming untied. But when I got to Ms. Hefflestine's room I found that she was still there, eating a live bat!

Just kidding!

It was a salad with fruits mixed in, which is almost as gross.

I lingered in the hallway, waiting for her to leave, but she never did. So, I missed lunch for nothing, hence Samwise munching on my warm PB and J.

Which also meant I had to implement Plan B.

Yikes.

So that's what I did.

Getting in trouble and earning a detention was easy enough. Mrs. Blotter has strict rules about showing up late to class. I told her I was in the restroom, which was true though I was just awkwardly waiting for the tardy bell to ring. She still slammed a detention on me. She even emailed my mom—by the way, I'm grounded this weekend, which is kind of a bummer, but was expected after I was forced to go with Plan B.

So, after school I found myself back in Mrs. Blotter's room sitting with a couple of other juvenile deliquettes—or whatever that word is. A boy with freckles named Tony, and Olivia, one of Usha's friends. I didn't know what they did to get such a sentence and I didn't ask. This wasn't pleasure or even punishment. It was something else.

The next step in my quest.

The four of us sat in silence. Mrs. Blotter at her desk grading papers and sipping on what I assumed was her thirteenth cup of coffee while Tony fought to keep his eyes open a few desks over and Olivia worked on homework behind me. For my part, I pretended to do homework while waiting for the right moment.

And the right moment came when, about halfway through the detention, Ms. Hefflestine popped her sister of Medusa head into the classroom to tell her fellow sister goodnight. I waited a few minutes, so I wouldn't rouse any suspicion, then pulled the contraband I mentioned in my last video from my pencil pouch.

Do you remember the parting gift the smelly kids at camp gave me?

That's right. The stink bomb. It was a plastic pill with a yellowish liquid inside. I dropped it on the ground beneath me and smashed it under my gym shoe like it was a nasty child of Shelob.

Shelob's a giant evil spider from *The Lord of the Rings*, in case you didn't know.

Though I was certain the stink bomb wouldn't help my reputation around Twin Valley Middle School, it worked.

The room filled with the smell of rotten eggs and Usha's friend, Olivia, gagged behind me and pulled the collar of her shirt over her mouth and nose.

Tony woke right up as if the stench had kicked him in the side. Gagging, he cried, "Yuck! What died in here?"

That caught Mrs. Blotter's attention. She leaned over her desk and her nostrils flared, before she cringed. "Uggh…" she said, all dramatic, "Tony was that you?"

And he was like, "No way, Mrs. Blotter, but someone needs to check their drawers."

I really wish Tony hadn't said that because I had to claim it in order for me to enact the next part of my plan.

Regretfully, I put on my best sour face and said, "Mrs. Blotter, ma'am, may I go to the restroom?"

Wearing a look of utter disgust, Mrs. Blotter waved for me to go.

And just like that, my reputation now includes the legend of me ripping off the biggest fake fart—or worse—in the history of Twin Valley Middle School.

Something tells me the elves of Middle Earth will not sing of it when I'm gone, but it's still worth it to me. I'd do it ten times over if it meant getting Ruth, Pappaw, and Hurston back to normal.

The deed was done and after a quick trip to the restroom so I wouldn't be totally a liar, I headed for Ms. Hefflestine's room. The door was shut and the lights off. I opened the door and quietly slipped inside. The door clicked loudly behind me.

I froze for a second or two before I regained my composure. Doing my best impression of a hobbit sneaking through the woods, I crept over to Ms. Hefflestine's bookshelf. The gray light of the cloudy day shone brightly enough through the window for me to see.

I was looking for the wizard's magic book. Thick as a mattress with a leather spine and gilded edges, it should've stood right out. But I wasn't stupid, a wizard wouldn't leave a grimoire just out there in the open. I was really looking for the perfect hiding place for a grimoire.

But I found nothing in the bookcase but books. I even pulled out each book as if one of them was a secret lever that would open a hidden door like in the movies.

No luck. I went to her desk. Snooping around another person's stuff was kind of icky, but if Ms. Hefflestine was the wizard, I had to find out. I opened her top drawer. Nothing but pencils and other school supplies. I checked the middle drawer. Folders of past assignments that were as scary as finding any grimoire. I tried the third drawer, but it was locked.

My muscles tensed. I was thinking the same thing you are right now: *That's gotta be it!* So I grabbed a paper clip, bent it out of shape and went to work trying to pick the lock.

That's when it happened.

The doorknob clicked behind me. Someone was coming in!

I panicked for a second. Two seconds probably, then I dropped down right where I stood and scurried under her desk.

The door shut and then footfalls came toward me. It wasn't the sound of heels clacking on the linoleum, so it probably wasn't Ms. Hefflestine. These footfalls were heavier and hurried.

Loafers appeared at the edge of my point of view, but I couldn't see their owner. Whoever it was, stopped by the bookshelf like I had and then moved to the desk. They tried the top drawer and then the middle and finally the third, discovering it was locked.

I still couldn't see the person and to be honest I was too terrified to move. My heart pounded. My stomach lurched. My skin prickled. I felt like the hobbits when they were hiding in the forest from the Ringwraiths.

I can't explain it, but I knew if this person caught me, I would be in serious trouble. And I'm not talking about detentions or being grounded or having a phone taken away. This person in the loafers was giving off some major danger vibes.

So I curled my legs against my chest and breathed as quietly as possible. The tips of the scuffed loafers were only inches away from the tips of my sneakers. Inches! And the room was so quiet and my heart against my ribcage so loud.

As I clutched my knees and silently pleaded for the stranger in the loafers to give up their search and leave, the stranger fiddled with the lock for a moment, then suddenly stopped.

My breath caught in my throat.

They heard me. I was sure of it! The *ba dum, ba dum, ba dum* of my racing heart was so loud—too loud.

But no. They heard something else and soon I did too. The clack of heels and the shrill sound of a sister of Medusa.

Ms. Hefflestine had returned, or was on her way. I could hear her talking on a cell phone coming up the hallway.

Surely both of us were caught, or at least the stranger in the loafers, but nope. The stranger stepped back to the corner of the room behind the desk, allowing me to see up to their waist, whispered something in a language I didn't understand, then—poof—vanished.

I'm not lying. The stranger disappeared.

They hadn't teleported or something, though. I studied the corner, wide eyed, when the light coming through the window shifted slightly, glimmering in the shape of a person. And that's when I knew.

The stranger was the same wizard Samwise and I followed from the library—the driver of the maroon car! Which means, the car had only vanished from my sight, not disappeared completely.

Ms. Hefflestine burst into the room in a flurry of conversation. She didn't notice the stranger. I could only hope she didn't notice me.

I didn't really catch much of what she was saying because she was talking fast and my gaze was locked on the corner of the room and the faint shape of a person standing there.

She went straight to her desk and the instant she turned her back on the shape, I got hit with a feeling I'd never felt before:

Fear for a teacher's wellbeing!

And not just any teacher, but a sister of Medusa.

I wanted to shout, "Watch out Ms. Hefflestine, there's an evil wizard behind you!" and was about to when I heard her say "lunch bag" and "under the desk."

My gaze slowly shifted to my left where Ms. Hefflestine's lunch bag sat a few inches away from me, hidden in shadow.

I was busted. She would certainly see me if she bent down to grab it—unless I acted fast. Without any magic trick to shield me, I did the only thing I could do: I reached over and nudged the bag out of the shadow to the edge where Ms. Hefflestine could easily see it.

My quick action worked. Ms. Hefflestine, prattling on unaware she was standing within arm's reach of an evil wizard, swooped down quickly and got the bag. I never even saw her face.

After Ms. Hefflestine left, my concern shifted back to the stranger. I could only hope the wizard hadn't noticed my little act with Ms. Hefflestine's lunch bag.

I sucked in another breath and held it.

The door clicked shut behind Ms. Hefflestine, leaving the room in mouse fart silence. Time slowed, or seemed to and every beat of my heart echoed in my ears. Seconds passed. Minutes maybe, and then the wizard revealed themselves, stepping out of their invisibility like they were stepping out of a shower.

The loafers came to a stop at the edge of the shadow under the desk, their tips facing directly at me.

I was a cornered animal. I squeezed my hands into fists, ready to...

I'm not sure what I was ready to do. Fortunately, I didn't have to do it.

The wizard took a step to their left and then, whispering in that same strange language, waved their hand over the locked drawer. The lock clicked and just like that, the drawer popped open. I wanted to steal a peek but I was still too afraid of being caught to move.

I know, not my bravest moment, but be kind in the comments. You didn't feel the wizard's danger vibes. I've got goosebumps just thinking about it. Look...

Anyway, whatever the wizard was looking for they didn't find it because they shut the drawer hard and mumbled, "Blast! I left it on her desk, where did it go?"

I know, right? Finally, a language I could understand.

The wizard crept to another part of the room. I didn't dare move too much but I shifted my weight from one side to the other as I followed the sound of their footfalls roving about. After what felt like an eternity, the wizard finally left the room, taking that horrible feeling with them.

I waited a minute, just to make sure they were gone, crawled out of hiding, then bolted out of that room like the devil out of church as my pappaw likes to say—errr—used to say...

When I got back to Mrs. Blotter's room, it was nearly time to be dismissed from detention. She didn't even bother to ask me what took so long. The stink bomb, the stench still lingering, was the reason for that.

So, Plan B worked, but when I was dismissed from detention and climbed to Mom's SUV, I had more questions than ever circulating through my head. The thing is though, as Mom backed the car out of her parking spot in the school's parking lot and went into lecture mode, I noticed something that caught my attention like a fly in one of the sticky traps that hang from the ceiling.

The maroon car belonging to the wizard was parked in the row ahead of us.

And that's not all.

But for the rest, you're going to have to wait.

All I can say is Holy Chocolate Cow! I know who the wizard is!

Ep. 17: And the wizard is...
Knighthood Never Looked So Good - 2,366 Views

Well, I got a new nickname.

Poopy Pants Paul.

Clever?

No. A kindergartner could've come up with better.

Stupid?

Yes.

But at least it's an alliteration.

No one said it to my face or anything. My classmates didn't encircle me with pointed fingers and chant "Poopy Pants Paul. Poopy Pants Paul." They probably whispered it when I walked by or called me it on social media.

I'm not friends with any of them so I only learned about it from Usha.

We just got off the phone.

After my discovery yesterday, I thought we should talk so I left her a note in a place I knew she would find it.

I'm grounded so I can't meet her at the tennis courts, and since there's already a rumor going around that I have a crush on her—for the record, I DON'T!—I decided it would be best to avoid contact at school.

Considering my newly acquired nickname, I think I made the right choice.

My dad answered the phone when she called. I had the cordless close by and he still beat me to it. He was in the basement office working so he probably thought it was a client. He rushed up the stairs with an extra pep in his step.

"Paul, there's a girl… on the phone for you," he said.

He looked surprised, but also proud in a way. I told him I'd get it on the cordless and Dad sort of tilted his head and gave me a curious eyebrow.

"She's just a friend," I said, though I could feel my cheeks blushing.

Don't read too much into that either. My cheeks blush all of the time. What can I say? I'm an easy blusher.

Anyway, back to the story.

With his dark shaggy hair, sky blue eyes, and sturdy frame my dad could pass for a ranger from the north. Mom said he was popular in college, so I imagine girls were flocking to him. That's definitely not the case for me and he knows it.

Still, Dad gave me a thumbs up and it made me feel kind of good inside. I grabbed the phone and ducked into our dining room.

Usha sounded somewhat apprehensive. She was like, "I got your note. I didn't even see you stick it in my tennis racket. Did someone help you?" And my stupid mouth replied, "No, I'm silky like that."

I meant to say smooth. Don't give me a hard time in the

comments for that either. I told you I don't have game or rizz.

Not that I would need rizz when talking to a girl who is just a friend.

Anyway, Usha was like, "Oh…" Then after an awkward pause she added, "So you think you know who took my homework."

I told her yes, but it was going to sound crazy and she chuckled and said, "Like your theory that an evil wizard is going around stealing pieces of people's souls."

And I was like, "Yes! Just like that."

Then she went quiet on her side and I told her I was being serious, and she was all, "That's what I'm afraid of."

At that point I glanced toward the basement stairs to make sure Dad wasn't listening, then I lowered my voice to a whisper. I told her I searched Ms. Hefflestine's desk. And she was like, "You searched Ms. Hefflestine's desk? How?"

I told her I grappled down from the ceiling like a superspy when the sister of Medusa wasn't looking.

Just kidding.

"Yes!" I actually said. "I got myself a detention yesterday and then used a stink bomb to get myself out of that detention just so I could."

And she was like, "So that's why…" before trailing off. When I asked what that meant, she hesitated then answered, "Ummmm… don't get mad at me but there's a rumor going around that you had an accident in Mrs. Blotter's room. People are calling you… Poopy Pants Paul."

I told her I expected something like that would happen and she asked if the nickname and the rumor bothered me. Which it does a little, because it's not true. But like I said, it doesn't surprise me. You don't drop a stink bomb in Twin

Valley Middle School and come out unscathed.

And it was worth it. Or as the Gaffer put it, "All's well that ends better." I assume most of you are aware of the quote, but if you're not, it's from *The Lord of the Rings,* and it means no matter how difficult the journey, if the destination is a better place, then it was all worth it.

After I explained that to Usha, there was another round of silence on her end, but this time it wasn't awkward. Then she said, "That's what I like about you, Paul."

My cheeks started to feel warm again and it was my turn to be silent. I bit down on the corner of my lip for a second or two because I did NOT expect her to say that. And she must've sensed it, because she then explained herself, saying, and I quote: "That you don't get caught up in all the popularity contests at school. You are yourself, all the time. As... interesting as that may be."

Did I memorize that? Hmmm...

"Anyway," Usha said after a few seconds, "you know who stole my homework." And I was like, "Yes, but bear with me..."

I then went into a vivid retelling of my escape from Mrs. Blotter's detention and how I hid from the wizard as he searched Ms. Hefflestine's room. Usha, for her part, seemed to be really listening. Which was a bonus because I wasn't sure if she would even call me in the first place.

After I told the story, Usha asked, "And you think this wizard turned my homework invisible?" And I told her, if he can open a lock with his words or turn a car invisible, then he can make her homework disappear.

It was a solid argument and Usha made no counterpoint. Instead, she asked, "Why?"

"Because he wanted to get me in trouble," I said and she was like, "So you think Levi is the wizard?"

Though Levi being an evil wizard wouldn't surprise me considering he stole my best friend, I answered, "It's not Levi, but it is someone at school."

Usha really wanted to know. I could tell it in her voice. She was like, "Who is it? Who?" And I was like, "Are you ready for this?" And she kinda whined and said, "Yes. Quit teasing me."

So I was like, "Okay. Okay." And then I took a breath, just to make her wait a second longer, because—being honest—teasing her was kind of fun. But finally, I told her what she wanted to know.

"It's Mr. Brindle," I said and she cried out, "Our principal! No way."

"Yes, way," I said back. "Yes, way indeed!"

And I could picture Usha shaking her head as she told me that Mr. Brindle lives down the road from her and that, "He's about as boring as they come."

And I pointed out just because he's boring doesn't mean it isn't him. Then she demanded to know what proof I had. And even though we were miles apart, I could tell she had her arms crossed.

So I explained myself.

One. The same maroon car that looks like it's from last century that drove by my house and disappeared in the alley in town was parked in Mr. Brindle's parking spot.

Two. The wizard is looking for something and he thought I had whatever it was. So, he needed a reason to search my things at school.

And that's when Usha interjected with this astude

observation.

She was like, "So he makes my homework disappear and conjures up a note saying someone saw you take it."

"Exactly!" I said back, squeezing the phone with excitement. "And now he has a reason to search through all my things."

Usha admitted that made sense, but she still thought I could be imagining everything.

I assured her I wasn't. But I did throw a lot at her, so I told her to take some time to think it over. In the meantime, I suggested we keep our distance from each other at school. And she was like, "Because if Mr. Brindle is a wizard, you don't want him to suspect that I know?"

I told her it was that and the whole Poopy Pants Paul thing and she laughed and thanked me for keeping her reputation safe.

And that's where our conversation ended.

So where does that leave us?

I got a new nickname.

Mr. Brindle is the wizard.

Now I have to figure out how to stop him and get back the pieces of soul he stole.

Ep. 18: An interesting discovery
Knighthood Never Looked So Good - 2,408 Views

Before I tell you about another interesting discovery that you're definitely gonna wanna hear about, I must address something. The internet vocabulary police busted me again. In my last upload, I said Usha made an "astude observation," and was corrected several times in the comments as the word I should've used was "astute," which according to dictionary dot com means keenly perceptive or discerning— And before you ask, I didn't look those words up...

My mom did it for me.

Anyway, I've decided to make "astude" a real word. From this point henceforth, "astude" shall mean keenly perceptive or discerning, while also meaning cool.

What do you think, Samwise?

BARK!

Samwise approves!

Okay, let's get back to the real purpose of this vid.

This time it was Usha who left me a note. I found it in my

math book. Here, I'll read it to you.

"Paul, I did some investigating of my own. It's not safe to tell you everything I found in a note, but I want to call you. Since I'm now grounded from my phone even longer, I have to wait until my step-mom gets home from work to use her phone to call you. She gets home around 5:30, so look for my phone call then. Bye, Usha"

My stomach was in knots, it took all my strength not to talk to Usha at school.

Not the bad knots you get when you're in trouble for something and waiting for the punishment but the kind you get when you're trying to sleep on Christmas Eve and all you can think about are all the presents waiting for you under the tree.

When I got home from school, I was so eager to talk to her I actually did my homework to pass the time. And when there was still an hour to go, I continued my ongoing construction of the Lego Millennium Falcon. It helped, but every few minutes or so I found myself thinking about her note and wondering what she had to tell me.

At 5:30, I had the cordless up in my room with me ready to roll, plus something else.

My parents' old tape recorder!

True to her word, Usha called at 5:35. I'm going to play you the audio of our conversation. Be warned, it's a little rough. This technology is older than social media. Alright…

Here it goes.

Click!

"Okay, tell me everything. Also, I'm recording this conversation."

"What?"

"I'm recording this conversation. You said you had something important, and I don't want to miss anything."

"Okay. Okay. Whatever. But we don't have long. My step-mom thinks I'm calling you for help with a math assignment."

"Two plus two is four. Math done. Let's talk."

"Alright... So, to be honest with you, after our conversation yesterday, I kind of thought you were letting your imagination run wild or something, but my dad came home in a terrible mood and we got into a big fight. After he stormed off to go work out, I got to thinking about what we read in the poem I found—"

"The soul reaver spell."

"Yes. I started thinking about it and how my dad's intensity and his temper has ramped up to another level lately and I'm not the only one who's noticed it. I heard my step-mom talking to Nani—that's my grandma back in India—about it. I don't want to get too far off track, but that's what made me want to find out if what you guessed about Mr. Brindle was true. So I snuck out and rode my bike down the street to his house."

"Did you see the car parked in the driveway or find a ratty old robe?"

"I didn't break into his house, Paul. I only watched it for a second from the sidewalk."

"Oh..."

"But I did see the car parked in his driveway. Funny thing, I never really noticed it before. According to my own research it is an '88 Chevy Caprice Classic."

"Eighty-eight as in 1988?"

"Yeah. You were right about the last century thing."

"Wow. What else did you find?"

"Nothing much. All the curtains were drawn so it was hard to see anything inside."

"Your note made it sound like something more. Is that all you found?"

"Definitely not, but it's not what I found, but what I observed."

"Okay. I'm listening."

"You know where I live, right?"

"Yeah. The fancy part of town."

"It's not that fancy. I mean, it's not like Serena Williams lives in a mansion next door. But I didn't call you to argue about what makes a neighborhood fancy."

"Right."

"Well, when I was at Mr. Brindle's house, I noticed a couple things that make me concerned. First, his yard wasn't mowed. I mean, it wasn't knee high or anything, but it was shaggy. There was already a written warning posted in the yard by our H.O.A."

"H.O.A? What's that?"

"Home Owners Association. You've never heard of that?"

"Oh yeah. Definitely, but we call ours something different."

Click!

Let me pause right there for a moment. First, before you say anything, I don't know why I fibbed about the H.O.A. thing. I'm not ashamed of our two-story farmhouse or anything like that, I just... I don't know.

Second, Usha made an astude observation as you will see.

Click!

"So Mr. Brindle's yard wasn't mowed."

"Yes, and after I noticed that, I decided to check his mailbox and guess what? It was full of unopened mail."

"Did you take it?"

"No, that's a felony, Paul. I don't want to go to jail."

"But it could've been correspondence with other evil wizards out there. Though I suppose evil wizards would probably use messenger crows or a magic stone. Or maybe just a cell phone. Hmmm... Does the devil offer a phone plan?"

"You're missing the point."

"And that is?"

"The yard needing mowing and the stack of unopened mail is evidence that Mr. Brindle hasn't been home."

"But his car was there?"

"Yeah, and he's not dead or anything because I saw him at school today."

"Hmmmm. This is getting weird."

"I know. What do you think it all means?"

"I don't know. But I think it confirms Mr. Brindle is our wizard since he's too busy hexing people to check his mail or mow his grass."

"So what do we do now?"

"Give me some time and we'll figure out something."

"Okay, but I hope it's fast because I don't want my dad to get so mad anymore."

"Me too."

CLICK!

And that's it. I didn't have the nerve to tell her what else would happen to her dad and anyone else who'd been hexed if we didn't find a way to stop Mr. Brindle. So, after she got off the phone, I went to work coming up with a plan.

Right now, I don't have much of one. Any help would be appreciated. Just leave your ideas in the comments.

Ep. 19: The start of a plan
Knighthood Never Looked So Good - 2,469 Views

I read your comments. Many of you had great ideas, so thanks for that. Also, as many of you pointed out, there is a lot to consider.

If Mr. Brindle is shredding souls as we suspect, then I must find a way not only to stop him, but also get the shreds of the souls back.

I've searched online and in my library books, but I've found no way to undo what's already been done. That really bothers me. I couldn't sleep last night thinking about it.

We all know what happens if we fail, but what happens if we stop Mr. Brindle but can't get the shreds of the souls back? What happens to Ruth, or Hurston, or Pappaw?

And Usha's dad?

Do they slowly fade until...

I don't even want to think about that.

There's gotta be a way. Think. Think. Think.

Bark! Bark!

Not now, Samwise.

Bark! Bark! Bark!

He wants to play fetch. Because that's what my dad does with him when he needs to think about stuff. They go out on the back porch. Dad tosses the tennis ball and Samwise leaps off the porch and runs after it. Dad calls it his thinking time, and it happens every night before the opening of a big case.

I'm impressed you recognized that I needed to think, Samwise. I've never thought you a fool, but you're smarter than I realized.

Bark!

Okay. Okay. We'll give it a try.

I'll be back.

Okay. I'm back with good news. Samwise is worn out, he's lying on the air conditioner vent by my closet, hopefully you can't hear him panting. And I have an idea.

Have you ever heard of a cease-and-desist letter?

It's like an angry letter that lawyers send out on behalf of clients threatening legal action against people who are using the client's stuff for their own personal gain. For example, a guy on YouTube made his own *Power Rangers* movie, but it was dark and violent and grown up. Nothing like the show we're used to. The original creator of the Power Rangers didn't like that so his lawyers sent a cease-and-desist letter to the YouTuber. The YouTuber mentioned the letter in another video and Mom and Dad filled in the rest so that's how I know what a cease-and-desist letter is.

If you haven't guessed yet, my idea is to basically send Mr. Brindle a cease-and-desist letter to tell him to stop what he's doing and return the souls or...

I'm not sure about the next part, but I'll think of something.

I'm going to run the idea by Usha and we'll go from there.

I'll let you know what she says.

Ep. 20: It's gonna be tricky-tricky-tricky

Knighthood Never Looked So Good - 2,464 Views

Good news. Usha's on board and we have a plan, but it's gonna be tricky.

We're going to give Mr. Brindle an ultimatum. Return the souls, or face the wrath of the Police, School Board, Parent-Teachers Association, Twin Valley Teacher's Union, Ohio National Guard, and the White Council of Rivendell.

Okay, that last one isn't technically a real thing but the others are, and I don't think they will approve of an evil wizard running their local middle school.

The problem, as Usha pointed out, is proof. Most people don't believe in wizards, especially adults. If we are going to convince Mr. Brindle to return the souls, we're going to need some proof as leverage.

Which means, Samwise and I have plans for later this evening.

Ep. 21: Caught in the Act
Knighthood Never Looked So Good - 2,994 Views

Samwise and I were camping in the backyard last night. At least that's what my parents thought when they peered out from their bedroom window and saw my tent aglow from the battery powered lantern I left hanging from the pole inside.

Of course, I didn't leave right away. I waited until all the lights in our house were off before Samwise and I made our daring escape. It was a little after eleven.

This was going to be a dangerous journey, so I brought some supplies that proved useful later. Stuffed inside my book bag was a pocketknife, two screwdrivers—one flathead and one Philips head—a flashlight, a blue Gatorade, and a container of iodized salt, which has been speculated online to act as a barrier to evil forces should the need arise.

It was a good hour's ride to Usha's neighborhood and Mr. Brindle's house. The night was warm and the sky clear with the stars dotting the darkness above me. Even though I've ridden my bike at night before, this was my first time alone as the other times Hurston was with me. Despite a nearly full moon providing enough glow that I didn't need my flashlight, I was still creeped out a little and I couldn't help but imagine every shadow or passing sound to have a sinister reason behind it.

Okay. I was more than a little creeped out, but the sweat that soaked my shirt and made it cling to my skin was from pedaling so fast. Mostly.

But Samwise was with me, riding in the bike stroller attached to my bike. And he would never let anything get the drop on me.

Would you buddy?

Bark! Bark!

That's a good boy. A good boy.

Samwise was heroic last night. Like for real! More on that later.

The bright orange glow of the streetlamps in Usha's neighborhood made me feel even more uneasy. If one of her neighbors took a peek outside, they would've easily spotted me. I had enough trouble with the wizard, I didn't need a police chase.

After a quick stop at Usha's where she left an old iPhone that no longer had a SIM card for me to use as a camera in her mailbox, I reached the end of the street and Mr. Brindle's house. It was shortly after midnight.

Just as Usha had said, the grass was tall, knee high for me—but Usha is taller than I am, so I'll give her a break on that—and the mailbox was still full of mail, I checked. The house was completely dark with the shades and curtains drawn.

The house—all quiet and dead—looked like a skull in the moonlight and it made the hair on my arms stand up, because in a weird way it felt like the house was staring back.

I got Samwise out of the bike stroller and ditched it and my bike behind an old truck parked in the driveway of Mr. Brindle's nearest neighbor. Usha had insisted it would be safe for me to leave my bike there because the owners were on a camping trip. Just to clarify, a real one in an RV. Not in a backyard tent used as cover for a clandestine stakeout.

If you're wondering, "clandestine" is one of my all-time favorite words. It means secret.

I slipped into the shadows and after what felt like forever, headlights appeared in the distance followed by the rumble of a diesel engine.

It was a rusty old truck. Three people were wedged in the cab. The truck pulled into Mr. Brindle's driveway, where it idled behind the maroon Chevy for a few minutes before the three men piled out.

I pulled out Usha's iPhone, pulled up the camera app, and hit record.

And here comes the first of many weird parts.

Two of the men were in pajamas and barefoot. I didn't recognize them. And the third was in his tighty whities and slippers! But I did recognize him. It was our school's maintenance guy, Phil, the husband of the lady I'd overheard talking in the library. It was like he climbed out of bed and decided to go on a road trip with two of his buddies.

One by one, they reached into the back of the truck and pulled out some tools. Phil grabbed a pickaxe while the other two grabbed shovels.

Unless they were trying to perform a live action roleplaying version of Minecraft, I knew what they were up to.

I leaned down to Samwise and said, "We're gonna go see what they're digging up. But we gotta be quiet."

I started to move but froze. *What if they're not digging up something?* I thought to myself. *What if they're burying something?*

The possibility turned my blood ice cold and I remained frozen until Samwise nuzzled my hand. I pushed that horrible thought aside and we darted across the road into Mr. Brindle's yard.

My muscles felt all loose and wobbly. Like when you're playing hide and seek and the person trying to find you is real, real close.

Going from tree to tree, we kept our distance from Phil and the other two men, but close enough to see them. We couldn't hear them too well, but they didn't really talk, just kind of grunted to one another.

We followed them to the backyard, which was a flat piece of land dotted with a few trees blocked in by thick woods at the rear. We took cover under the dangling fingers of a weeping willow. A garage lay to my left and a garden to my right.

Speaking of the garden. My pappaw would've pitched a fit if he saw it. It really needed some tending. A few thistles had sprung up and many of the crops were wilted and dead. That was another oddity, considering there was a water hose attached to a sprinkler spanning the distance between the garden and the house. Just add that to the growing list of weird things about Mr. Brindle's home.

Back to the story. I expected the men to start digging but they didn't, they just stood there, shovels over their shoulders. I kept the camera rolling anyway, until Samwise perked up suddenly.

Something in the woods at the edge of Mr. Brindle's backyard seized his attention. His ears went rigid and a tuff of hair on the back of his neck bristled.

"What is it, boy?" I whispered.

Samwise growled low. I placed my hand on his head to let him know not to be loud. He must've understood my meaning because he didn't growl again, but he didn't move either. He didn't even blink. His stare was transfixed by something in the shadows. I squinted at the dark and for the briefest of moments I thought I saw the profile of a large animal moving through the tree line and then the glint of green eyes. And that's when the next strange thing happened.

Usha's iPhone vibrated, interrupting me and drawing my attention away from the woods. The camera had automatically shut off. I turned it back on and when I looked back up, Mr. Brindle was striding over to the three men. Fortunately, he wasn't in his skivvies like the others. He wore his shirt and tie like always. Another oddity I didn't consider until right this minute.

Hmmmm...

Anyway, now left in a state of confusion, I glanced over at Mr. Brindle's house. It looked the same as before. The back door was shut, and the porch light was off. I'm still not sure where he came from. I could hear him walking through the tall grass the same as the other men, but I didn't hear his approach. It was like he—poof!—appeared in the yard out of thin air.

From our hiding spot next to the trunk of the weeping willow, Samwise remained still, unblinking, while I squatted lower into the tree's shadow.

Phil and the other two men bowed to Mr. Brindle as he approached them. Mr. Brindle said nothing but made a gesture toward a nearby garage located at the back end of the property. Like they were robots or something, the men turned in that direction and marched in a line over to the garage. Phil opened the door and all three disappeared into the dark followed by Mr. Brindle. A few minutes later, Samwise and I heard the sound of metal smacking against rock.

Crack! Crack! Crack!

I kept recording but there wasn't much to see because no one had turned any lights on inside the garage. The sound of the men's hard work continued, and I kind of expected them to break out in song like they were a chain gang or the dwarfs from *Snow White*.

If this were a Tolkien tale, they definitely would've sung a song. But this isn't a Tolkien tale and my lyrical capabilities have been pretty much maxed out by trying to guess the words of the soul reaver spell.

And this is a modern tale, so if there was to be a song, it would be a sick diss track released on Spotify or YouTube.

Eventually, I leaned down to Samwise and whispered, "There is definitely something strange going on here, but I don't think this is enough evidence to convince Mr. Brindle to return the souls. We need something concrete. We need to know what they're digging up in that garage."

I knew they could be burying something, but my stomach knotted up even thinking about that.

Samwise looked up at me, the first time he'd moved since we thought we saw something in the woods.

"We need a distraction," I said.

Samwise spun in a circle then stopped on a doggy dime, peering in the direction of the garden.

"Great idea, Samwise!" I whispered, and I rubbed his ears as a thank you.

And it was a good idea, so without hesitation I scurried over to Mr. Brindle's house. Keeping an eye on the garage, I crept along the outside wall until I got to the spigot. After giving it a few seconds of thought, I decided just turning on the sprinkler wouldn't be enough. I needed them out of the garage, but I also needed time to investigate. The solution came in the form of the flathead screwdriver I brought in my bag of supplies.

"Let's hope this works," I whispered as I stuck the screwdriver through the gaps on the spigot's handle. "One. Two. Three."

Using the screwdriver as leverage, I turned the handle with all my might. I yanked and yanked and yanked and finally, the handle snapped off. The rush of water through pipes sounded from within the house before the water hose filled with life and like a snake slithering through the grass, took aim at the garden.

With the head of a sprinkler, the snake spit its venom with a hiss that you've all heard before.

Tis. Tis. Tis. Tis. Tisssssssssssssssss.

In the middle of a quiet night, the sprinkler's hiss and the sound of its venom smacking the ground and plants in the garden was loud and obnoxious.

"It worked!" I whispered to Samwise. "Now run!"

And we did. We booked it back to the weeping willow and ducked behind it.

Sure enough, Phil and the other two men came barreling out of the garage followed by Mr. Brindle. They surveyed the scene, their sweaty foreheads crinkled in confusion. For his part, Mr. Brindle didn't look confused, but annoyed. Without a word, he gestured toward the spigot and the three men lumbered over to it.

I caught a glimpse of Phil's face that sent a chill crawling across my skin. His cheeks were slack and his eyes were the color of eggshells, solid and pupilless. I thought instantly of Phil's wife's words in the library.

Zombies.

I shuddered.

She was right. And if I don't find a way to stop Mr. Brindle, will Ruth, Pappaw, and Hurston end up like that? Was Usha's dad already one? Can that explain how extra intense he's been lately?

Hmmmm... Back to the story.

I needed to find out what they were digging up in that garage. But Mr. Brindle stayed behind, watching his eggshell-eyed servants from the entrance, and I thought my plan had failed. However, when the three men were unsuccessful in turning off the sprinkler, Mr. Brindle shook his head and stomped over in their direction.

I pumped my fist in triumph. "It worked, Samwise," I whispered. "Now I'm gonna go have a look. You stay here, watch my back."

And I left him there, as I crept across the lawn into the darkness of the garage. Where I found—

Knock. Knock. Knock!

Paul, can I come in?

Hold on a second, Mom.

There's a girl on the phone for you.

There is?

Oh shoot. It's Usha.

Hold on guys, I'll be back.

Ep. 22: I found something!
Knighthood Never Looked So Good - 3,001 Views

I apologize. I know I said I would be right back but my conversation with Usha went on a little longer than I expected as I detailed for her what happened last night, and then we talked about some other stuff that didn't have much to do with wizards or anything. I think Usha needed a listening ear and honestly, I didn't mind at all. I won't go into what we talked about. That definitely wouldn't be a cool thing to do and a violation of the Paladin Knight's Code of Honor.

Anyway, back to last night.

I told Samwise to stay by the weeping willow and I slipped into the garage. The moonlight shining through the open door painted a small portion of the garage floor with a bluish color and glinted off the metal casings of power tools and saws that had been shoved to the edges of the garage.

My heart pounded like a jackhammer. I didn't have much time. But the moonlight wasn't bright enough for me to navigate the garage, so, I did the only thing I could do, I turned on the light on Usha's iPhone. After scanning the area quickly, I cupped my hand around the iPhone, doing my best to limit the light to the floor in front of me.

Three sets of muddy prints led away from something in the dark of the garage. I followed them and nearly fell into a deep hole! Teetering on the edge, I regained my balance and shined the light down inside. The hole wasn't cavernous like the Mines of Moria, but it was pretty big and looked deeper than I was tall. Just behind the hole was a pile of dirt and chunks of busted up concrete.

I made sure to get a good shot of it then aimed the iPhone's light directly down into the hole. I won't say I was looking through the gaps in my fingers, but I wasn't keen on finding a dead body.

Fortunately for me and my stomach, something else protruded from the bottom of the hole. A ginormous wooden chest with steel hinges and an oversized keyless lock.

At this point, you're probably wanting video evidence of this. Well, I hate to disappoint you, but you will have to wait on that until I know it's safe to upload.

I know. I know. Many of you will see my resistance as proof I'm making this all up. I promise you, I'm not. But go ahead and vent your frustration in the comments. In the words of Gandalf the White, "Haters gonna hate."

Okay. Gandalf didn't say that. But that's the motto of the day.

Back to last night.

Though my heart was racing and I sensed my time was running short, I had to see what was in that chest. I had to. It was kind of like having to pee in the middle of the night or seeing a really cool movie trailer. There wasn't a voice speaking to me or anything, but an urge compelling me. So, I gave one last look to the open door behind me and climbed down into the hole.

The ground was mushy under my shoes and the air was strangely thick, like when we are having one of Pappaw's mosquito nights—that's when an extra muggy day makes the air feel like soup.

There was no time to waste, so I didn't waste any. Shining the light of the iPhone onto the chest, I hurried over to it and knelt. As I got closer, I noticed something. You know how when a big thunderstorm is rolling in and the hairs on your arms kind of stand up like they can feel the electric fingers of the storm reaching out? Well, that's kind of how I felt. And the sensation got stronger the closer I got to the chest. It made my stomach churn too.

On closer inspection, the chest was just like any old treasure chest you'd see in a pirate movie, but the lock was something else. There was no key, but also no combination or number pad. In other words, there was no obvious way to unlock it. However, there was some bizarre writing embossed on the front the lock. And here comes another strange thing.

When I first looked at the lock, the writing was written in a foreign language and I definitely couldn't read it, but when I looked at the lock a second time, it was in English. I kid you not. I made sure to get a good shot of it with Usha's iPhone before I read it out loud, but real quiet so Mr. Brindle wouldn't hear. Here's what it said.

If you're wondering, I wrote it down as soon as I got home.

"Of which no intention to keep, will this bond allow to seek. And once found, they will be bound. If the words you can read."

And just as I finished reading the words—*CLICK!*—the lock opened. I'm not going to lie. I stumbled backwards, startled, and fell right on my butt. I know, at that point I should've expected it but still…

I stood up and dusted myself off. Lifting the top of the chest, my eyes went wide. And to find out why, you're going to have to tune into my next video.

Just kidding!

It was the book Mr. Brindle had when I first saw him in his ratty bathrobe in the woods behind the Swafford's burned up old house. The grimoire.

The same aged leather. The same gilded edges. The same gold writing. But now I could read the entire title and I did.

"*Absalom's Key*"

At that moment, I felt a shift in the air—a drop in the temperature. Pappaw's mosquito night had been touched by Jack Frost. I went still and rigid. Afraid to even shiver.

Somehow, I knew. I can't explain it, but I knew. I wasn't alone. I was in danger.

I hadn't heard him come in. No footsteps, no whispering under his breath, no heavy breathing. But Mr. Brindle was above me. Sniffing at the air as he peered down into the hole.

With my back to the garage door, I couldn't see him, but I could sense him. He was there, just a few feet away from me. *Sniffing. Sniffing. Sniffing.*

Somehow, he couldn't see me, but I didn't dare move, even when a bead of sweat tickled my spine as it drained down my back.

Seconds passed that felt like hours before I heard footfalls and grunts coming in my direction. Mr. Brindle was soon joined by the zombies. My ruse was up.

I glanced down at the grimoire and to my astonishment, I saw a mirror on the cover reflecting my face but also the silhouettes of Mr. Brindle, Phil, and the other zombies above me. They huddled around the hole with their shovels and axes.

Mr. Brindle's eyes narrowed to slits with suspicion, then he nodded. I didn't hear the command, but on his cue, the three men raised their tools as if they were spears and prepared to plunge them into the hole. Doubting whatever magic or trick of the shadow was shielding me from their sight would protect me from their shovels and pickaxes, I swallowed hard and prepared to leap out of the way.

And that's when the bravest, most loyal dog a boy could have sprung into action.

Samwise burst into the garage barking and growling like a dog three times his size. A blur of fur, he circled Mr. Brindle and his goons. They grumbled and howled, taking haphazard swings at him. When Samwise dashed in front of him, Phil took a shot from another goon's shovel on the top of the foot that caused Phil to drop his pickaxe and leap around, grabbing his foot while yelping in pain. Chasing after Samwise, another of the zombies tripped over something and knocked himself out cold on a chunk of concrete. The third man got himself tangled up in the table saw's power cord. Mr. Brindle was the last one standing, and he didn't look pleased.

Samwise stopped and squared himself between me and Mr. Brindle. Samwise growled and Mr. Brindle hissed at him. Before Mr. Brindle could make a move, Samwise darted between his legs. Mr. Brindle attempted to grab him, but the surprisingly slippery Samwise slithered through his grasp and bounded out the door. Mr. Brindle let out another strange hiss and dashed after him, surprisingly quick for a man his age. Seconds later, the other conscious zombie and

Phil joined in the pursuit, limping.

Samwise gave me a chance!

I had plenty of footage, but I could do even better, so I turned off the iPhone's camera and stuffed it and the grimoire into my bag. And that's when the last strange thing happened—the last strange thing so far anyway.

Well, having everything I needed, I shut the chest, but when I did so, I felt the weight of the grimoire vanish from my bag and the lock reappeared with those same foreign words again. Disappointed that I couldn't keep the grimoire as evidence against Mr. Brindle, but knowing I didn't have much time, I settled on the footage and climbed out of the hole as fast as I could.

Doing my best impression of the Flash, I sprinted through Mr. Brindle's backyard, stopping by the goon's truck in a moment of inspiration to slash their tires with my pocketknife, and across the street to my bike.

I climbed on my bike and rode like the wind, trusting Samwise would remember to meet me at home.

And he did.

But for the most anxious hour of my life sitting on the steps of my front porch, I wasn't sure he would.

I'm not kidding. I was worried sick, like for real. You can check my mom's flower garden in front of the porch.

Basically, what I'm saying is, if my hair turns gray by the time I'm twenty-one, I'm blaming you, Samwise.

Now come here, so I can give you a hug.

Ep. 23: Cease and Desist!
Knighthood Never Looked So Good - 3,441 Views

Okay. Everything is ready.

Usha and I worked on the message over the phone. I cut out letters from Mom's old *People* magazines and glued them to a piece of paper, which made me feel like a serial killer in a police show on TV, but oh well.

After I uploaded the footage from Usha's iPhone to my laptop, I took screenshots of certain images from what I filmed last night, printed them out, and tucked them into the envelope with the letter.

I know this is technically blackmail even though I'm calling it a cease-and-desist letter, but what choice do I have? I mean, can you think of a better way to convince Mr. Brindle to give back the shreds of soul he's taken? Normally, with just a plain ole' cease-and-desist letter, we would threaten to sue him, but I don't think there's a supernatural law court out there. And I doubt any law firm would take on a case against a wizard.

So the plan is set, and everything is ready. After school tomorrow, on her way to the tennis courts, Usha will stick the envelope on the windshield wiper of Mr. Brindle's car. And then we wait.

And as they say, "The waiting is the hardest part."

Ep. 24: ...
Knighthood Never Looked So Good - 3,654 Views

Guys, this isn't good at all. I'm worried sick and I don't know what to do.

I was sitting in Mr. Macadoo's Social Studies class working on a WebQuest when a new email popped up. I minimized the WebQuest and pulled up my email. The sender was unknown and the subject read *"For the Meddler."*

Before I even clicked on it, I got a sick feeling in my gut.

I glanced around the room. No one was watching me. I took a breath to calm myself then opened the email, hoping my instincts were wrong and it was just spam.

My instincts definitely weren't wrong. I wish it would've been anything other than what I got. A Nigerian prince asking for money! Tips for unlocking the stock market! An extended warranty for a car I don't own! Actual canned spam!

Nope.

It was a simple message.

"Return what you took from us or face dire consequences."

With a picture of Samwise below it.

I didn't have to fake sick to get out of class because I threw up right there. On the floor next to my desk.

I didn't tell Mom about the email when she came to get me from the nurse's office. All I could think about was Samwise. When I asked if he was home, lines formed between Mom's eyebrows and she said, "He should be, but I came here straight from work."

I bit down on my bottom lip, grabbed Mom by the hand, and hurried us out to her SUV. Outside, I noticed Mr. Brindle's car wasn't in his normal parking spot, but when I looked up toward his office window, I caught him peering at us before he closed the blinds.

I know who sent the email. And it makes sense. I was on my school account which restricts email to only people in the network.

But I wasn't too worried about that. All my worry was for Samwise.

"We need to get home fast," I urged Mom. "Okay. Okay," she said, turning the key in the ignition. "But if you feel like you're going to throw up, just let me know and I'll pull over so you can… you know."

I chewed on my nails which is something I never do. When we got home, I scrambled out of the car before Mom even turned it off, ran up the front steps, used the key hidden under the flowerpot, and threw open the front door, calling for Samwise.

I waited for something. Anything.

The sort of yelp he makes when he yawns after a long nap.

His bark.

The click of his paws on our wood floor.

But none came.

Guys. Samwise is gone.

Ep. 25: Can it get any worse?
Knighthood Never Looked So Good - 3,847 Views

Things have gone from bad to worse.

I searched everywhere for Samwise, foolishly hoping he'd just gotten outside somehow and ran off chasing a squirrel. Mom was worried about him too. When I returned from searching our neighborhood, she and I drove up and down the roads calling his name.

It was no use. There was no sign of him anywhere.

Eventually, Mom asked why I'd been worried Samwise was missing even before we got home.

Rubbing tears out of my eyes, I pulled up the email on my laptop.

Mom pulled the car over, snatched the laptop off my lap, and leaned in intently, her face shifting from worry to even deeper concern.

"It's from Mr. Brindle," I told her. "He's a wizard and he's been hexing people. Samwise and I went to his house over the weekend to get some evidence and—"

That's where she cut me off, insisting she had to call Dad.

She did and put Dad on speaker phone and he was like, "Any luck on Samwise?"

"We've been all over," Mom told him. "There's no sign of him anywhere." And Dad asked if we thought Samwise had got to chasing something, like a cat or a squirrel, but Mom was like, "No, I think someone took him. And I think it has to do with the Jones case."

I could picture Dad's brow beetling together like it does when he's surprised by something. "What?" he asked. And Mom explained about the email I got from school. When Dad heard that, he got as angry as I've ever heard him.

"They're going after my kid now!" he growled. Then he told us to head to the sheriff's office, that he would get Ruth from school and meet us there.

Squeezing the steering wheel until her knuckles turned white, Mom drove as if we were being chased by the Ringwraiths, her attention bouncing back and forth between the rearview mirror, the side mirrors, and the road ahead. The ride was tense and quiet, until Mom broke the silence.

"Did you see any suspicious looking people at school today?" she asked me. I told her, "Mr. Brindle," but she shook her head and said she meant people I didn't recognize or someone who didn't look like they fit in. I said no and she asked about the bus stop. I shook my head and answered, "Samwise saw me on the bus like always, but I didn't see anyone suspicious. I was the only one there."

Unless that person was invisible. Darn it!

"And he was home when I left," Mom added before sinking into deep contemplation, the edges of her face bent by worry.

Dad and Ruth were waiting at the sheriff's station when we pulled in. Dad threw his arms around me and said, "We'll get Samwise back, Paul. Okay. We'll get him back."

Then all four of us rushed into the station, which wasn't much more than a small office building. Sheriff Daniel Whaley came out of his office as soon as we entered. Sheriff Whaley, with his kind eyes over a thick dark mustache, looks like the sort of desperado you'd see in a cowboy movie, but with a gut that hangs over a big silver belt buckle.

In his booming voice, he was like, "John, is everything all right?"

I didn't know Sheriff Whaley but Mom and Dad did, through work I guess.

Dad answered his question then asked if we could all talk in his office. Sheriff Whaley gestured us toward his office, and we filed in with Dad leading the way. Sheriff Whaley sat down at his chair.

His office was the opposite of Mr. Brindle's. Mr. Brindle's was neat and tidy in a way that made you feel cold all over. Sheriff Whaley's was vibrant and disorganized. A mounted bass hung on the wall overlooking a desk cluttered with papers and keepsakes.

"So what's the situation?" the sheriff asked, and Dad answered, his tone all flat and serious. "It's the Jones case."

Sheriff Whaley's eyes narrowed a little and was like, "I thought you weren't concerned about the threats, said it's nothing new on a big case like that one."

And that's when Mom chimed in and said, "We weren't until our dog went missing." And the sheriff was all, "The corgi I see running around with your son sometimes?"

And I was like, "His name is Samwise!"

I'm not sure why I did that. I guess I didn't like the way he made it seem like Samwise was just "some" dog. But *we* know Samwise isn't just some dog. Still, Mom gave me a stern look for talking to Sheriff Whaley that way.

After Mom and Dad assured him Samwise didn't just run off, they both looked at me and Dad said, "Paul, show him the email." And I did, while also trying to explain that it had nothing to do with the Jones case but with Mr. Brindle.

But they all ignored me.

The sheriff slipped a pair of reading glasses on his nose and leaned forward. He studied the email for a moment real hard, then said, "I see you got this email at 12:17 this afternoon. Is that correct?" I told him I was working on an assignment for Social Studies when I got the notification. "And there wasn't an ID on the email anywhere?" he followed. "No sir," I said. "Only the unknown address. But I know who sent it."

Sheriff Whaley scrunched his thick eyebrows together like he was really ready to hear me out. I know what you're thinking! Finally, someone was willing to listen to me. Or so I thought.

"And who is that?" he asked. And I told him. "Mr. Brindle, my principal. He's a wiz—"

And that's when Mom interrupted me. "That's enough, Paul," she said. "This isn't a time for your fantasy worlds. This is serious."

But I was being serious! I said, "Mom, he took Samwise and I want him back."

And I could feel the tears coming...

I didn't want to cry in front of the sheriff. I really didn't. But I couldn't help myself. The thought of...

Give me a second.

After I started crying, Sheriff Whaley said, "Whoever took him, we'll do our best to get him back." He looked at Mom and Dad, tapped my laptop, and added, "Our tech guy is a kid fresh out of college. He's good with this stuff. If there's anyone who can figure out who sent this email, it's him."

Sheriff Whaley grabbed the laptop, saying he was taking it down the hall to their tech guy, Lidell, and that he would send a deputy to come in and take our official statement.

The sheriff disappeared down the hall. I focused on the sound of his boots fading away to stop crying. That and knowing that he was going to help find Samwise.

A moment later, Deputy James stepped into the office with a special pad of paper. As my Pappaw would say, Deputy James was skinnier than a string bean and looked young enough to be a high school student. He asked me a bunch of questions and wrote his answers on the paper. Dad and Mom weren't happy to hear me accuse Mr. Brindle again and when Deputy James left, they let me know about it.

Mom was like, "Paul, I know you have a very active imagination—and we love that about you—but you can't go around accusing people of kidnapping your dog." And Dad chimed in with, "That's slander, son. That's a crime." And I was like, "Words are only slander when they're made up. But I'm not making this up. This is true. Mr. Brindle thinks I stole something from his garage over the weekend, but I didn't."

And now I wish I could take that last part back, because parents never miss those things.

Dad peered at me for a moment, then was like, "Wait? You

went to Mr. Brindle's house this weekend? But you were ground—You were on the backyard campout."

I bit down on my bottom lip. Busted.

Then Mom hit me with a flying jump kick from the top rope. "Yep," she confirmed. "Paul, snuck out."

And Dad's nostrils flared he was so mad. He was all, "So not only did you disobey us, but you trespassed as well."

And I tried to defend myself. I was like, "I know it sounds bad, Dad. But I had to. Mr. Brindle's a wizard."

And Dad was like, "He's *not* a wizard, Paul. They aren't real." Then I came back with, "They are and Mr. Brindle is a bad one. He's been hexing people, stealing pieces of their souls."

Then Ruth, who'd remained quiet the entire time, decided it was her turn to take a shot at me. She took that accusing tone she's had with me lately and said, "Paul, this isn't a real good time for one of your stories." And I was like, "This isn't one of my stories, Ruth. This is true. He's hexed you and you don't even know it."

Then Ruth flashed a glare at me and was like, "What are you talking about?" Then Mom and Dad joined Ruth with their hostile glares, making me feel really outnumbered.

So I was like, "Why are you looking at me like I'm crazy? You know what I'm talking about. I've heard you talking about how you're worried about her. How's she changed."

Which is true, I overhead them two nights ago in the living room when I was loading the dishwasher after dinner.

Well, Ruth didn't like that very much. Her face turned pink and she looked at Mom and asked, "Is that true?"

Then Mom told her I was just confused and taking things out of contacts. Which didn't make sense because I don't even wear glasses, let alone contacts.

Anyway, I said, "I'm not confused. It is true! You've changed, Ruth. You're all wrapped up in yourself now." And she was like, "No, I'm not." And I was like, "Don't lie! I saw you in the mirror. All you care about is how you look. Remember when I walked into your room and caught you talking about how ugly and fat you think you are?"

And that really set Ruth off. Her eyes flashed and she lunged for me. Luckily, Mom stepped between us, or I might be talking to you from the other side right now.

I could tell Ruth was burning up with anger. She blew out a breath, told everyone she was going to the car, and stomped out of Sheriff Whaley's office before anyone could protest.

Dad started to get up, but Mom tugged on his arm, telling him to give Ruth a moment, but Dad left anyway, saying he would give her space, although he was still going to keep an eye on her.

That left me alone with Mom.

I know.

Yikes.

Well, a few seconds of thick silence passed before Mom pinched her nose and sighed. "I know you're worried about Samwise, but you can't say things like that about your sister."

Mom was probably right but I couldn't keep it to myself, so I let it all out and said, "But it's true. Ruth doesn't want to do any of the cool stuff with me that she used to do. And she's not the only one. Hurston has changed too. He pretty much hates all the stuff he used to love and he won't even hang out with me anymore. And there's Pappaw."

Mom asked me what was wrong with Pappaw and I said, "Last time I went to see him, he acted as if he didn't know me or Samwise. He chased us out of his room, Mom. He said…

He said… we were going to get him killed!"

And that's when the pipes behind my eyes busted open. The tears came in big heavy drops down my face. I tried to stop them, but I couldn't.

Through wet cheeks and a sniffling nose, I said, "I know you don't believe me about Mr. Brindle being a wizard, but everyone around me is changing. All the good things are being taken away and if I don't do something…"

And at that moment, something seemed to click inside Mom. The anger and frustration faded from her face and she began to cry too. She motioned for me to come close to her and I did. She wrapped her arms around me. Holding me close to her chest, she told me she knew how I felt.

Then she revealed some stuff that's filled me with doubt ever since.

She said, "Ruth is in those awkward teen years where it's so easy to get down on yourself and that wasn't helped when someone posted a mean-spirited picture of her on social media while you were at camp."

I let out a small gasp at that. Because of my stunt in detention and the homework thing with Usha, I knew a little about how Ruth felt—the embarrassing loneliness of knowing everyone is talking about you for the wrong reasons. And I may have just made it worse. My stomach twisted up with a mixture of sadness and guilt.

But Mom wasn't done talking yet. "Your father and I do worry about her. As we worry about you."

Then I asked about Hurston and Pappaw, because neither of them is in their awkward teen years. And she answered, "Hurston is into new things now. That happens. Sometimes friends drift apart. And Dad—I mean—Pappaw. We should've told you about him. It's a hard thing for me to come to terms with too."

I was confused. I didn't know what she meant about terms.

"A term paper?" I asked before Mom chuckled through a sob and said, "No, I'm not talking about a term paper. Pappaw didn't fall and break his hip while checking the mail. He had an episode caused by a disease called Alzheimer's that affects brain function. He's forgetting things more and more and sometimes he has flashbacks to his time in Vietnam."

I nodded because that did make sense with what Pappaw said the last time I saw him.

Then Mom apologized for not telling me, saying something like, "You and him are close, and sometimes as a parent you think you have to shield your children from everything that will make them sad."

After she said that, Mom's lips quivered, which means shook, like she was a concrete dam about to break. And it only got worse when I asked if Pappaw would get better.

I really hoped she'd say yes. Pappaw is the only human who really seems to get me.

But a big fat tear streaked down her cheek as she shook her head and I couldn't help but cry more too. For Mom. For Pappaw. For my best dog, Samwise.

Eventually, Mom rubbed my head and said, "I know you have a lovely active imagination and this is a lot to take in, but you're growing up and a big part of that is learning to handle changes, even when they make you sad." But I told her good things shouldn't change and she squeezed me tighter and said, "I know. But sometimes they do and you can't help it. All you can do is appreciate what you had."

Then she asked if I understood what she was saying.

I nodded.

I did understand and maybe I did get what was happening to Pappaw, Ruth, and Hurston wrong. And probably Usha's dad, too. But Samwise was still gone, so I asked her about him.

She said it was most likely someone working for the plaintiffs in the Jones case. They think my parents' clients, and by extension my parents, stole from them after the court made their initial ruling.

I don't know much about the Jones case, but the Jones family owned a mansion not far from town and were the richest people around. I understand why they would be mad losing to Mom and Dad in court, so Mom made sense.

But what about the disappearing car and everything else I saw Friday night at Mr. Brindle's? I couldn't be imagining all of that, could I? I mean, I had footage.

Before I could ponder it further, Sheriff Whaley returned with Lidell, the department's tech guy. Sheriff Whaley rapped at the door frame with his knuckles and said, "Pardon me, Mrs. Weaver, but may we have a word with you in private? Lidell here wants to show you something."

Mom dabbed her cheeks with a tissue from a box on the sheriff's desk and stepped out into the hallway. The three of them had a short, whispered conversation with Lidell pointing to something on my laptop before Mom turned around to face me, her expression contorted by confusion or maybe it was shock.

Then Sheriff Whaley peered at me, his face going all serious and said, "Son, I'm going to ask you again. Who sent this email to you?" And I told him again that I didn't know, the sender was unknown. Then he said, "If that is true, then why does the sender's I.P. address match your laptop?"

See, from bad to worse.

Ep. 26: I did not see that coming...
Knighthood Never Looked So Good - 4,501 Views

I know I cut you off there in my last upload, but I didn't know what else to say.

Samwise is still gone.

Gone!

And the police think I made the whole thing up and my parents think I've let my imagination run wild or worse. Maybe I have let my imagination run wild, I don't know.

I denied that it was me who sent the email from my laptop. I explained that our school limits emails to people who are part of the network, and my laptop isn't on the school network, so it shouldn't be possible. Lidell agreed with me, but he's looking into a way I could've got around it.

To prove I wasn't lying about Mr. Brindle and *Absalom's Key*, I tried to show them the footage I recorded. It took lots of pleading but when I pulled the files up after they finally caved, I got an error message saying the file had been corrupted and was unable to open. I even tried to pull up the footage on Usha's iPhone but got a similar error message.

I know it's not unheard of for files to become corrupted, but the timing was more than suspicious!

I pointed that out and Sheriff Whaley said in his booming voice, "Son, you know making these kinds of accusations is a big deal. A big no-no."

"First," I wanted to say, "I'm not your son, so stop calling me that. And I'm not a little kid, so no-no on out of here."

Of course, I didn't say that, Mom would've killed me. But I was also kind of shaky. I felt like I was in one of the rooms in a cop show with the two-way mirrors and bright lights where the detectives try the good cop, bad cop routine—except everyone was playing the role of bad cop, even Mom.

Sitting there I was like, "I'm *not* making this up. And I didn't send that email. You think I would kidnap my own dog?"

Sheriff Whaley just shrugged and countered, "Son, we've seen all kinds of things in this office." And I was like, "How about a car turning invisible? Have you seen that? Or three men in their underwear digging a pit in the floor of someone's garage in the middle of the night?"

At that moment, Deputy James, who'd been listening from his chair at the front desk, piped in and suggested they call the school's maintenance man and see what he was up to that night.

I told them not to call Phil because he wouldn't remember because he was hexed and instead, they should call his wife.

Deputy James picked up the phone and was like, "What do you say, Sheriff?" And the Sheriff sighed and said, "I suppose it's worth looking into."

Deputy James dialed, held the phone to his ear for a long time, then hung up. Apparently, no one answered, and her voicemail was full. He did promise to try again later, but as of this recording, I haven't heard if he was successful yet.

Then Sheriff Whaley said he had an idea. Then he looked at Mom and asked if he and Lidell could have a moment with her.

Mom nodded and her, Sheriff Whaley, and Lidell stepped out of the office, closing the door behind them. I could see their silhouettes through the foggy glass, but could not make out what they were saying.

I took the time to pray—in hopes of getting Samwise back and to prove I wasn't going crazy.

When the door finally opened, Dad had joined them. He gestured at me and was like, "Come on, Paul."

When I asked where we were going, he wouldn't tell me. Dad's expression was stern, but also racked with disappointment. It made my stomach sink seeing him look at me like that.

I stood up and said, "I didn't take Samwise."

But Dad didn't respond, he just walked to his car, and I followed.

We climbed in and sat for a moment with the car idling. It appeared neither of us knew what to say. Sheriff Whaley climbed into his cruiser and Dad finally put the car in gear once Sheriff Whaley got his cruiser moving.

It didn't take me long to figure out where we were going. And when I saw Mr. Brindle in his front yard, dressed in usual school attire, checking his mailbox, my suspicions proved correct. Just seeing him made my blood boil like hot lava. I wanted to leap out of the car and demand he return Samwise.

But Dad stopped me with a hand over my chest and a sharp command to stay there as he pulled his car to a stop behind

Sheriff Whaley's cruiser.

Dad climbed out of the car and approached Mr. Brindle with Sheriff Whaley. And for a moment, I thought they maybe were going to arrest him.

But those hopes were dashed when Sheriff Whaley smiled and tipped his hat. It was also at that moment I noticed Mr. Brindle's yard was mowed almost to perfection. My stomach shifted uneasily.

Dad didn't look nearly as friendly as the sheriff. He crossed his arms as they spoke.

I wasn't allowed to get out, but that didn't mean I couldn't listen to their conversation, so I rolled down my window and tilted my head out the window toward them, cupping my hand around my ear.

Sheriff Whaley was all, "Their dog is missing, and the son believes he might be here. Do you mind if we look around?" And Mr. Brindle was like, "Sure thing, but I don't know what would make Paul think his dog is here."

Then Sheriff Whaley said, "Just humor him," which made me mad because there's nothing humorous about Samwise being missing.

Mr. Brindle nodded and Dad motioned for me to get out of the car, and I did so, jogging up to him. All of us walked around to the back side of the house.

Now, this next part I couldn't tell if my dad was just trying to be nice or if it was part of a strategy to catch Mr. Brindle.

Dad admired the yard for a moment then said, "Yard looks nice," and Mr. Brindle replied, "Yep. Mowed it Friday after school before I headed out for the weekend."

So I locked my accusing gaze on Mr. Brindle like I was the Millennium Falcon's targeting system because the yard definitely wasn't mowed when I was there Friday night.

Or was it? Am I really going crazy?

Anyway, Mr. Brindle was at least lying about being out of town all weekend. I definitely saw him there, even if I couldn't access the footage to prove it.

At least I think I did.

Back to it. Dad wasn't done with Mr. Brindle yet. He asked him where he went and Mr. Brindle was like, "Fishing trip with some old college buddies. We go up to Lake Michigan every year." And Dad was like, "Sounds like fun. And when did you get back, exactly?"

And that's when Mr. Brindle stopped suddenly and was all, "Am I in some kind of trouble here?"

Sheriff Whaley assured Mr. Brindle he wasn't and that, "Mr. Weaver here's just making small talk." But even though Dad nodded his agreement with the sheriff, I knew his questions weren't meant to be small talk or whatever. He was questioning Mr. Brindle like he would cross examine a witness on the stand in court.

It made me feel a little better that Dad was at least considering my side of the story.

We continued walking, though Mr. Brindle had yet to make eye contact with me. We reached the backyard.

I surveyed the yard, garden, and tree line, calling for Samwise. Dad gave a whistle. And everyone stood still for a moment, listening. I clutched at the edges of my shirt, hoping to hear the sounds of Samwise's footfalls and the clinging of his collar tags breaking over the chirp of the birds and late summer cicadas.

But I didn't.

"Samwise!" I yelled. "I'm here, boy! I'm here! Let me know where you are!" And Mr. Brindle was like, "I don't know why the dog would be here. Never seen him here before."

And Sheriff Whaley peered down at me as if to say, "See, I knew you were making everything up."

And I was about to tell him off when Dad said, "What about the garage? Could he have gotten in there somehow?"

That's when Mr. Brindle flashed a look of pure bewilderment and was like, "My garage was locked all weekend, I don't know how—" Then Dad cut him off, insisting we have a look just in case. And before Mr. Brindle could respond, Dad was heading toward the garage.

Mr. Brindle looked at Sheriff Whaley and I could tell he wanted Sheriff Whaley to stop my dad from going in, but Sheriff Whaley said, "It won't hurt nothing to have a look." And Mr. Brindle flashed disappointment, maybe even a little frustration, as he fished out a set of keys from his pocket. He really didn't want us to see what was inside his garage.

I jogged to catch up to Dad, anticipation and hope building inside me. When I got to him, he was already peeking through one of the windows. I jumped up to have a look, too, but all I got was a glimpse of woodworking equipment.

Sheriff Whaley and Mr. Brindle reached the door and Mr. Brindle said, "I really don't know what the point of this is. My garage is locked all of the time. I hardly even go in here." But Sheriff Whaley suggested we have a look anyway before promising we'd be out of his hair soon.

Mr. Brindle reluctantly unlocked the door and was all, "Please don't touch anything. My tools are dangerous and expensive." Then he stepped through the door first and flipped a light switch. Dad and I went inside next, followed by the sheriff.

My hopes were dashed to pieces.

The garage was nothing like it was Friday night. The tools and machines were neatly spaced out, not shoved to the side. The floor was clean and pristine with absolutely no evidence of a pit being dug in the middle of it just a few days before.

I shook my head. It was impossible. Impossible!

Dad crossed his arms, scowling.

And Mr. Brindle got all smug and was like, "See, your dog isn't here." And I frowned deeply and I could feel the tears prickle my eyes as I considered that maybe my imagination had run wild or…

But I was struck with an idea before I could consider it any further. I cried out, "Wait!"

And remembering the alley where Mr. Brindle's car had disappeared and what happened in the sister of Medusa's classroom, I said, "This is just an illusion!"

And Mr. Brindle snapped, "What? That's crazy."

And I was like, "That's what you want everyone to think, but I know the truth."

Then I stepped outside the door and grabbed a rock about the size of my fist from the gravel walkway leading to the garage and added, "This is all fake. There's a pit right in the middle of the floor and I'm going to prove it."

I raised my arm to throw the rock like this… and Sheriff Whaley was all, "Don't throw that, son," and Mr. Brindle was like, "I'd listen to the sheriff if I were you." Then even Dad chimed in as well. "Paul, don't!"

But they were too late. They needed to see! So, I tossed the rock, sure it would break through the illusion and fall into the pit.

But it didn't.

It clanged off one of the saws and bounced to a stop on the floor.

There was no pit. There was no illusion. My mouth fell open as I slunk my shoulders forward in a mixture of confusion, disappointment, and shock.

To make things worse, Mr. Brindle put his hands on his hips and snapped at my dad, saying, "Mr. Weaver, control your son!"

And if Dad were a cartoon, steam would've been shooting out of his ears, he was so mad. He peered at me and with clenched teeth said, "Go to the car, now!" And I started to protest but a swift gesture toward the car cut me off.

I didn't dare talk back again. I know better. On the verge of crying once more, I shuffled back to the car, confused about how wrong I was.

Dad eventually came back to the car, still stewing with anger. He didn't say a word the entire drive home and neither did I. Dad barely even glanced in my direction.

When the car ride was over, Dad peered forward, still unable to look at me, and said, "I don't know if you lost Samwise somehow and you don't want to get in trouble or if you're trying to pull a prank on your principal. Or if this is a cry for attention. But we will get to the bottom of it. Until then, go to your room and stay there."

So that's what I've done. And I have no clue what to do now.

My parents think I'm crazy. Ruth is ultra mad at me and won't talk to me. I can't call Usha and worst of all...

Worst of all.

Samwise is gone.

And whoever took him thinks I have *Absalom's Key*. But I don't. It definitely isn't in my bag.

What kind of Paladin Knight-in-Training am I?

Maybe all that stuff is fake. The pursuit of justice. The code of honor. Fake. All fake.

Or maybe I'm just crazy.

But I don't think I am. I don't.

But all I have as proof I'm not making everything up is this stupid iPhone with corrupted video files.

This no good, worthless iPhone!

Ugh! Take this!

Ouch!

What the?

Did you guys see that?

I threw the iPhone and it came back. Hit me right in the chest.

Maybe I am seeing things. I better check to make sure. Let me rewind. Hold on a sec.

That. Was. Weird.

It definitely happened. But let me try again.

Take this iPhone!

Whoa!

Did you see that? Please tell me you saw that?

All right. I'm going to try it for a third time. And maybe this time I'll catch it.

On three.

One. Two. Three.

Gotcha!

Wait? What's this? I didn't see this app on here before.

Oh my...

Does that say?

Holy Chocolate Cow! You guys won't believe this!

There's a new app on Usha's iPhone.

Here look.

That's right. Absalom's Key.

Let's see what happens when I open it.

Whoahhhhh...

Hello, Paul, I've been waiting for you.

It spoke!

Wait?

How did you know my name?

I better check this out.

Ep. 27: Help me Ruth, you're my only hope
Knighthood Never Looked So Good - 4,786 Views

Ruth! Ruth! Open up. Please.

Go away, Paul!

Please.

I'm not ready to accept your apology!

Just open the door. There's something I have to show you!

I don't care! Go away!

You have to see it! It's about Samwise!

Click!

You have ten seconds.

Thanks for opening the door.

Ten seconds, Paul, get on with it—Wait! Why do you have your laptop with you? Are you filming this?

Yes. I need video evidence of what I'm about to show you.

Okay, whatever. You have ten seconds.

Okay. Okay. You're probably going to think I'm crazy, but I need you to hear me out. What I said about Mr. Brindle is true.

Not this again.

It is. And I have proof. Here look at this.

An old iPhone? How is this proof?

It's not the iPhone itself. It's this app.

An app that looks like a book? How is some app proof?

Absalom's Key isn't really an app. It's a grimoire. A very powerful one.

A grimoire, like a book of magic?

Yes!

That's enough of this game, or prank or whatever this is. You said this was about Samwise.

It is! I'm not crazy. You think I'd hurt Samwise or put him in some kind of danger just to play a game or pull a prank on Mr. Brindle? Samwise is the only friend I have left. He's...

Sorry, Paul. I wasn't saying—

Everyone else is. I went downstairs to show Mom and Dad first, but I overheard them talking about me in the living room. They think something may be wrong with me. That's why I came up here. I knew they wouldn't even listen, but you would.

I don't know if I should. I mean, you told everyone I was selfish.

I'm sorry for that. I thought someone stole your soul. I didn't know you were going through teenage stuff.

Yeah, well, it hurt my feelings.

I'm sorry. I really am.

Okay. Now, show me the app.

Can I come inside?

Yes.

Creak. Click.

Thanks. Can I sit my laptop on your desk?

Sure.

Thanks.

So what does this app do? Does it let you access satellite cameras or something like that?

No, nothing like that. But I gotta give you some background first.

This has become a long ten seconds.

I know, but you will understand in a minute. Anyway, this all started when Samwise and I went to see the Swafford's old place after the fire department burned it down for practice. While we were there we heard some strange chanting and Samwise took off into the woods after it. I caught up to him and that's when we saw Mr. Brindle dressed in what looked like a ratty old bathrobe standing over one of those stone piles you see in a children's illustrated Bible.

An altar.

Exactly! He was standing over an altar with a fire on top chanting a spell while holding a large leather-bound book in his hands, before he saw us and we made a quick escape. After some investigation, I discovered the book was a grimoire and that Mr. Brindle used a "soul reaver" spell to take shreds of people's souls for reasons I still don't know. At least, I thought he did... Anyway, fast forward to this last weekend when Samwise and I staked out his house and discovered him using hexed town members to dig something up in his garage. And when I got down in the hole to see, I found this like treasure chest and inside it was the grimoire—*Absalom's Key*—the same book Mr. Brindle had in the woods... Are you keeping up?

I think I got the gist of it. But I have a question, many actually, but my first is why didn't you record it? I mean, you record everything.

I did, but the file got corrupted somehow.

So you have no proof?

Not until now.

You mean the app. How do you know that's not some coincidence and that I can't just look it up on the App Store?

I tried. You won't find it anywhere.

Okay. What does it do?

That's what I wanted to show you. Check this out.

Shalom, Paul, baloka shev.

Besides your name, Paul, I didn't understand a word of that.

What do you mean? It said, "Hello, Paul, welcome back." How'd you not understand that?

Other than your name, it sounded like a bunch of gibberish.

Hilell hillolave all vino ti.

What do you mean, she can't understand you? I understand your English just fine.

I mena debil sa vadica.

An old language? Hebrew? Then why can I understand you?

Meshum shev a sidda do shevah.

Because I turned the key? But there was no key for the lock on the chest—Oh wait. The inscription!

What inscription, Paul? What's going on?

I'm still trying to figure it all out, Ruth. But when I found the chest in Mr. Brindle's garage, there was an inscription on it that read *"Of which no intention to keep, will this bond allow to seek. And once found, they will be bound. If the words you can read."*

What does that mean?

I think it means I was able to open the chest because I wasn't interested in keeping the grimoire.

Nakhon!

The app says I'm right.

Okay, what about the second part, the "once found they will be bound," part?

I'm not sure, but I think it's because I opened it up and read a little bit.

Hold on! Let me see the iPhone.

Okay, here.

What does that say?

A Seeking Spell for finding lost things.

In English?

Yes.

But I don't see English. I see something that looks like calligraphy or Latin. Unless you're making it all up.

I'm not, I swear.

Prove it, then.

How do I do that?

You see my air pods?

Yes.

Now step out of the room for a minute.

Why?

Because I'm going to hide them.

Okay?

Click!

Click!

Okay, Paul. If you're telling the truth, then you can use that seeker spell and find my earbuds.

I'll try but…

Do or do not, there is no try.

Thanks, Yoda.

You're welcome. Now go and prove you aren't a crazy liar.

Okay. Here goes everything. Absalom's Key, show me the seeker spell.

Lifequdatekha, adonay.

Here it is. I must look and listen, for what was lost can be found by listening for its sound.

Hear that, Ruth?

No. Hear what?

The sound of your music.

That's impossible. I turned my phone off. See?

Well, I hear it, which means... One of the earbuds is in between your mattress and box spring and the other is... in your back pocket.

Holy Chocolate Cow, Paul! You aren't lying.

I told you.

So what do we do now?

We get Samwise back.

Ep. 28: The calm before the Storm.
Knighthood Never Looked So Good - 4,812 Views

Okay. We're live.

I'm documenting this so that if anything happens to us, someone will have an idea where we went.

That's a scary thought. But I don't know what to expect.

I didn't charge my laptop enough so hopefully what battery life I have will last.

It may be hard for you to see in the evening light, but I'm here at the park again. Ruth snuck me out of the house and drove me here. Well, she drove us here.

She's on her phone right now. She had to cancel her plans with her friends tonight.

Usha's on her way too. I used Ruth's phone and called her. I told her I might be wrong about the soul reaver spell and her dad, but after I explained the situation with Samwise, she insisted on helping us.

And here she is.

Usha!

Hey. I came here as fast as I could.

Thanks for ummm… showing up.

No problem. Samwise needs our help, right?

Yep.

And you have a plan?

Yes.

All right, let's hear it.

We're going to give Mr. Brindle what he wants.

You're going to give him the grimoire? Didn't you say he was a dangerous wizard?

He is, but it's the only way to get Samwise back.

I'm not sure this is a good plan.

You didn't let me finish.

Shouldn't your sister be hearing this too?

No, she already knows the plan. She helped me come up with it.

Oh. Then let me hear it.

I've been talking with the app's A.I. which explained a lot of things to me and taught me a few spells.

Wait—The app has an A.I.?

Yeah, but it's complicated. I mean, only I can understand it for some reason and before you ask, I don't know why.

Okay… Are you sure you're not hallucinating? I don't want to be rude but…

I'm not and I can prove it. You have a flashlight with you?

Yeah. It's in my bag.

Get it out and turn it on. Oh! You may want to put those sunglasses on too.

Why?

You'll see.

Okay...

Now watch. *Kalah Kadoom!*

Whoa, Paul! That would've blinded me!

Only temporarily—I made that mistake already—It's like a magical flash bang but the spell only works if there is an external source of light.

So the spell doesn't create the light, only manipulates it?

Right. From what I can tell, that's how most of the magic in the grimoire works. But now that I've convinced you I'm not hallucinating, do you want to hear the rest of my plan?

I guess.

Okay, I'm going to hand the grimoire over to Mr. Brindle so I can steal his soul.

Wait! What?

I'm going to steal Mr. Brindle's soul.

You can't do that!

I don't have a choice.

But it's not a good idea.

It may not be but I can't think of a better one. If I'm understanding the grimoire correctly, Mr. Brindle has used the soul reaver spell, just not on the people I suspected. Why he's doing it, I don't know but the only way to undo the spell is to shred Mr. Brindle's soul.

Yeesh... but why do you have to give him the grimoire? Can't you just do the spell?

Because the spell requires an exchange. You give something to get something in return.

So all of the people he's hexed into zombies received something from him?

Yes. And they probably didn't even know it.

Why is he doing this?

That's a great question. I asked the A.I. and it didn't know.

Then how do you know for certain he used the soul reaver spell?

That website where I originally discovered the spell wasn't exactly accurate. Or at least didn't tell the whole story. One of the reasons a sorcerer would use the spell was to gain control of another person. According to the A.I. it's subtle at first but over time the hexed person begins to show symptoms. Strange mumblings and eggshell eyes, for example, before they...

Before they what?

Before they eventually die.

Whoa. This got dark.

Yep.

So not only do we have to get Samwise back, we have to find a way to save the people he's hexed as well.

And we don't know everyone who's been hexed by him. I saw three the other night, but there could be others.

Okay, so your plan is to steal Mr. Brindle's soul by exchanging the grimoire for it. What's going to keep him from using the grimoire on us once you hand it over?

Because I'm not going to give him the actual grimoire. I'm not that dumb.

If Mr. Brindle is this powerful wizard, won't he know the difference?

Nope, because the grimoire takes on a different form for each owner, something that will make it easier to understand and also camouflage it, I guess.

I get it. A book for him and an app on an iPhone for you.

Yeah.

I still don't know about this, Paul. I mean, if we fail...

I know, Usha. I'm not a huge fan of this plan either, but right now we have leverage.

You really think we have the upper hand?

Not exactly, but we have two advantages. One, we have what he wants. Two, a grimoire is the source of the wizard's power and he doesn't have the grimoire so—

So this might actually work.

Have you told her the second part of your plan?

I'm getting there.

You must be Ruth.

And you must be Usha.

Yes. Ruth meet Usha. Usha meet Ruth.

Are you and my brother, like, a thing?

Ruth!

What? It's a fair question, Paul.

We aren't a thing. I'm not even allowed to have a boyfriend.

See Ruth, you don't even need to bring it up. And there's much more important things to deal with right now.

Okay. Okay. Tell Usha about the second part of the plan.

Yeah… ummm… stealing Mr. Brindle's soul is only half of the battle. Once we have it, we have to shred it without killing him. And we do that by finding a vessel to put it in.

What do you mean by a vessel? Like a jar or something?

According to the app, it's got to be something personal to him, an object he cares a lot about.

Something he's attached to, something that has sentimental value.

Right, Ruth.

Okay, why don't we go to his house and find something, like a family heirloom?

We already have a vessel in mind. Something everyone knows he cares a lot about. And it's not at his house. The problem is getting it.

And that's where you come in, Usha.

Okay… Your tone makes it sound kind of bad. Is it?

Depends. Have you ever dreamed of being a cat?

Ep. 29: I can't believe it's come to this.
Knighthood Never Looked So Good - 5,008 Views

I'm going to steal my principal's soul.

I get it. It sounds crazy and definitely evil. Don't get the wrong impression about me, though. I'm not crazy or evil, though there is crazy *and* evil in this story.

I'm just a concerned citizen. And I didn't come to this decision lightly. I came to this decision *heavily* because someone I care about is in danger. Like for real danger. Like the forever-dead-as-a-door-nail kind of danger.

And I have to help him.

If you're new to my channel, you're probably wondering what my principal did that led to this drastic decision. Well, I don't have time to recap now, so you'll have to watch my previous uploads.

Whether you watch the videos or not, wish me luck. I'm gonna need it.

If I pull it off, you'll know, because I'll be right here posting another video.

And if you don't see me again... Well, I guess you know what that means.

This is Paladin Knight-in-Training, Paul Weaver, signing off.

Ep. 30: Bad News Part 1
Knighthood Never Looked So Good - 5,432 Views

Is this thing on?

Yes? No?

Yes!

Hello, everyone. As you can tell, I'm not Paul. I know I've been on here once or twice and Paul's talked about me—too much about me—but I've never like officially been introduced as far as I can tell.

My name is Ruth. I'm his sister. I didn't expect to ever make one of these recordings—nor wanted to—but when I finally found my brother's channel and saw all the questions in the comments in response to his last post over a week ago, I decided it was best if his loyal followers found out what happened.

Paul would want that.

So, I'll do my best to tell you what happened and I'll try... I'll try not to get too emotional.

Bear with me though. It's been a long seven days.

And apparently, the website only allows videos to be uploaded in thirty minute or less segments or something like that, so this entry may come in parts. I don't know. But anyway.

So, before Paul even recorded the last video, he'd received another email from that unknown address demanding he show up at his school at midnight with the grimoire to exchange it for Samwise. That's when we formulated—or made—our plot.

If only it had gone as expected. If it had, then Paul would be the one talking to you right now, not me.

But I can't change that. I can only tell you what happened.

When we arrived at the school, at least two people stood at every entrance. Each carried a weapon of some sort—a garden hoe, a shovel, etc. One lady had a curling iron. My gym teacher, Mr. Lade, was one of them. And he was holding a baseball bat. They stood completely still, unblinking, their eyes white like eggshells, just as Paul described.

My blood ran ice cold and I felt like the air in the car was firming up around us. I'm kind of ashamed to admit that, but up to that moment, I didn't fully believe or grasp what Paul had said.

I didn't think he was lying. I mean, I saw the app and what the grimoire allowed him to do, but... I don't know. Seeing is believing. And the way they just stood there, so rigid, it was so unnatural. The scariest Halloween decorations ever. If only they were Halloween decorations.

I was about to call the cops when Paul pointed and said, "Don't."

One of the sheriff's deputies—the skinny one—stood by the

side entrance to the cafeteria with Ms. Hefflestine, his hand resting on the handle of his gun.

I tucked my phone back into my pocket, then asked how he expected us to get in there. And Paul was like, "If Mr. Brindle wants the grimoire, he'll let us in."

Then, from her perch on the center console of my car, Usha said, "What about me?"

Another moment of confession. I will never get used to hearing a cat speak.

Okay, anyway, Paul answered her, saying, "You're going to follow us inside, but be all sneaky about it." And she was like, "Then I go to Mr. Brindle's office and grab the vessel?"

Paul nodded and told her she'd want to break the spell first, before reminding her of the words.

Proinde parce mihi transformatio. Or something like that. They practiced it so many times, I should have it memorized myself.

Then he reiterated she shouldn't say it until she's ready or we'd have to find another cat to trade places with. And at that moment, the cat—in Usha's body—curled up across the back seat, purred.

Which is a strange sound coming out of a human.

No worries, we didn't hurt the cat. We gave her a big bowl of warm milk in hopes the experience for her was no more than a strange dream.

After that, Paul explained the rest of the plan to Usha for like the fifteenth time. Saying, "Once you have the vessel, place it on the floor and draw a circle with chalk around it. And then write these symbols on the circle where the cardinal directions would be on a compass."

Usha nodded that she understood, then Paul slipped a

rolled-up piece of paper with the symbols drawn on them through a loop on Usha's—the cat's—collar.

With that taken care of, I asked if we were finally ready and Paul was like, "I have the fake grimoire, A.K.A. my *Lord of the Rings* encyclopedia." Then Usha added, "I have the paper with the symbols on it."

And I had pepper spray and a whistle in my purse.

With that we started to get out of the car, but then Paul stopped us.

"Wait!" he said. "I just realized something." And Usha and I snapped our attention to him, panic having seized both of us—or at least me. And then he was like, "We're kind of like *The Fellowship of the Ring*."

Ugh. My brother! He never stops... He never stopped being him. The eternal geek.

Anyway, I snapped at him, "That's it? I thought you were going to say we forgot something important." And he was like, "The Fellowship is important."

And the whole time Usha stared at us with blank green eyes because she had no clue what the Fellowship was.

So I told her the Fellowship was from *The Lord of the Rings.* That they were the people who set out to destroy the evil ring. Then she immediately asked, "Ummm... Did they all survive?"

And Paul and I looked at each other, before he said, "Okay, forget I brought it up. May the odds be ever in our favor or whatever." Which I pointed out, also wasn't a good choice.

And with that we climbed out of the car. Usha hopped out after us, darting away into the shadows, her silky black fur acting as the best camo. As we approached the main entrance, I caught a glimpse of Usha's shiny eyes in the dark.

Is it possible for a cat to look nervous? Because she did.

Or maybe it was just me projecting on her.

Guarding the main entrance was the maintenance man, Phil, and his wife. Phil wore a walking boot on his right foot and had a skillet while she had a mop. Paul strode right up to them with me in tow.

Paul held up the book and declared, "We're here to speak with Mr. Brindle. I have Absalom's Key."

Phil and his wife stood unmoving. Paul waved his hand in front of their faces, and they didn't even flinch. Paul stepped back, looked at me, and shrugged.

Then, a deep inhuman voice boomed in unison from both of their mouths: *"You may proceed, but know, we will be watching."*

Phil and his wife opened the front doors and stepped to the side. I swallowed hard and followed Paul inside.

Without saying another peep, the zombies marched us down the hall. The school was mostly dark aside for a few safety lights that I guess stay on all the time. Before we rounded the corner, I glanced back to make sure Usha got in safely. Her green eyes shone from the shadows behind us. Phil's wife nudged me with her mop and pointed. I got the message and kept my eyes forward the rest of the trek.

The zombies led us to the gym and I gasped when we stepped inside. The lights in the gym were off, the scoreboard was dark, but the room was lit by a multitude of eggshell-eyed zombies standing in the bleachers holding lit candles.

It was like the whole town had fallen under Mr. Brindle's control. I surveyed the crowd, my mouth gaping. There were many familiar faces, neighbors and teachers but no kids. I don't know the reason for that. Anyway, fortunately, Mom and Dad weren't among them, but my friend's mom was and so was Usha's dad. Like the other zombies, they stood completely still, not making a sound at all.

At center court, where the jump ball would take place if we were starting a basketball game, a bunch of rocks had been piled up to make an altar of some kind. A shiver crawled down my spine when I saw the stack of wood on top of it. The image brought to mind the Bible stories I'd heard in Sunday school about pagan sacrifice. I won't go into details, but they never ended well.

Mr. Brindle stood there, dressed in an elegantly ornamented robe. It wasn't the ratty bathrobe Paul had described him wearing before. Maybe he got a new one? Or something else was going on.

The zombies herded us to center court.

Mr. Brindle's hawk-like eyes surveyed us, then asked, "Do you have it?"

Paul cleared his throat. If he was nervous, he didn't show it.

Anyway, Paul told Mr. Brindle he had the grimoire, but he wouldn't hand it over until we had Samwise back. And Mr. Brindle regarded Paul for a moment, then said, "Show me the Key." And Paul didn't hesitate. He was like, "Show me Samwise."

Mr. Brindle's eyes narrowed behind his thick glasses. I think he was surprised by the courage Paul was showing.

Mr. Brindle gestured to one of zombies standing by the equipment closet in the gym and said, "Very well then."

The zombie pounded on the door. It opened seconds later, and another zombie stepped out leading Samwise by a leash and choker chain. Poor Samwise was muzzled and sad, but he perked up real fast when he saw Paul.

Seeing Samwise like that really lit a fire inside Paul. He clenched his jaw and demanded Mr. Brindle let Samwise go.

But Mr. Brindle just held up a finger and was like, "Ah. I said you could see him. You can have him back when I get my Key."

Paul held fast. Even after I leaned over and whispered, "Give it to him."

Paul was eager to get Samwise back. His courage hadn't gone anywhere, but his expression was hard like stone. I didn't realize at the moment that he was stalling to make sure Usha had enough time to perform her part of the plan.

Mr. Brindle did little to hide his impatience. He sneered, "I would do as the young lady suggests." And Paul countered, "Not yet. I have some conditions."

Mr. Brindle didn't like that very much. He let out a small gasp and clutched at his chest all dramatic and was like, "Conditions? How can you make demands from me? I have your beloved pet." But Paul came back with, "I have Absalom's Key. And I've been reading it."

That's when Mr. Brindle arched a long eyebrow and was like, "Reading it?" Then Paul pointed at him and said, "Yes, and the protection spell YOU put over it, now extends to me. Therefore, you can't take it from me. I have to give it to you."

Mr. Brindle's eyes narrowed again, this time into a glare. He fumed, "Don't press me, Paul. I will do what I have to."

Then Paul inhaled and exhaled slowly. His anxiety over Samwise poked through his determined expression before he said, "No, you won't. Because if you hurt Sam in any way, I will destroy the grimoire."

Mr. Brindle scoffed at first, saying Paul wouldn't, but Paul was like, "I would. I know the spell. I found the words on the grimoire's own pages."

I wasn't sure if Paul was telling the truth, but it didn't matter, because Mr. Brindle believed he was. At least the grave glint in Mr. Brindle's eyes made me think so.

Mr. Brindle's hard stare lingered on Paul for a few tense seconds, then he sighed, "Fine, what are your conditions?"

With that settled, Paul listed his conditions.

"First," Paul said, "you return all of the souls you've shredded and free all these people. Second, you free Samwise. And third, you leave this town and never come back."

Mr. Brindle crossed his arms at the list and was like, "You ask a lot of me." And Paul responded with, "I didn't ask." And he crossed his arms as well.

Mr. Brindle was quiet for a moment, before a twinkle of inspiration sparked in his hawk-like face. He peered at Paul and laid it on thick: "You've shone a lot of spunk, Paul, I'm quite impressed." But Paul saw right through it. "Don't try to flatter me," Paul said. "I'm not going to fall for any of your evil wizard tricks." But Mr. Brindle came back with, "Who said I was evil?"

And that's when I cut in. Gesturing to the zombies in the bleachers, I was like, "Duh, look around."

I mean, it was pretty obvious.

Mr. Brindle didn't think so, however. He frowned and said, "Don't be so dramatic, dear. I didn't steal their souls, I'm only borrowing them. And I can assure you, it is for the most noble of reasons."

At that point, Paul was starting to get impatient. He was like, "Do you accept the conditions or not?" And Mr. Brindle snapped his focus back to Paul and asked, "If I do, I suppose you intend for me to keep my word by binding me to an unbreakable vow?"

Paul's face went blank for a moment and Mr. Brindle followed with, "Have you not read that spell in the grimoire?"

Paul answered with, "Of course," but he sounded a little too defensive. And Mr. Brindle seized on it, saying, "Then we agree to terms," before holding out his hand and adding, "Now for the unbreakable vow."

Paul stared at Mr. Brindle's hand with apprehension, while my stomach flipped over.

Mr. Brindle gestured toward Paul and was like, "You may have forgotten, as you've been so busy reading, but in order to complete the unbreakable vow, we must link hands."

Paul nodded, then took Mr. Brindle's hand and Mr. Brindle's expression somehow became even more serious as he met Paul's gaze and said something that sounded like *"Ut sive nobis morti juramento."*

I waited for a spark or a clash of a cymbal or something, but nothing happened, and Mr. Brindle broke off the handshake before gesturing for the zombies holding Samwise to bring him forward.

They did as directed, holding Samwise back as he fought to get to Paul. Then Mr. Brindle reminded Paul of his end of the bargain and Paul went to work unzipping his book bag. He pulled out *The Lord of the Rings* encyclopedia and held it solemnly in both hands.

Mr. Brindle's eyes went wide with hunger as he whispered, "Finally." But when he reached for it, Paul yanked it back and said, "Release Samwise."

With a simple, "Very well," Mr. Brindle nodded and the

zombies holding Samwise removed the muzzle and choker chain.

Samwise bolted to Paul, who dropped down to his knees and captured Sam in his arms. A lot of face licking and tail-stump wagging ensued before Mr. Brindle interrupted the reunion by clearing his throat.

Paul stood and Samwise turned and growled.

Mr. Brindle looked pointedly at them both and said, "Now, Mr. Weaver, the Key."

Breathing deep, Paul slowly extended the book. Mr. Brindle seized it from his hands like a spoiled kid snatching his newest toy from a playmate. "Yes! Yes! Yes!" Mr. Brindle cried. "We've waited so long for this."

Paul glanced back at me, indicating it was time, then began to chant, *"Reponere senex dot com novum, Ray Romano filum, consuno et add,"* or something like that. I don't know the wizard language.

Anyway, Mr. Brindle, who'd been grinning gleefully, puckered his face and was like, "What? I recognize the words! You're trying to shred my soul!"

And Paul finished the incantation and then responded with a triumphant smirk of his own.

But that smirk faded when Mr. Brindle's cheeks reddened with rage. He sneered, "Liar!" then held up the book and said, "This is a fake!"

And with that, *The Lord of the Rings* encyclopedia burst into flames! It was like the fire reflected the anger flickering in Mr. Brindle's eyes! "Seize them!" Mr. Brindle cried. "Seize them!"

As if awoken early from a long slumber, the army of zombies scrambled from the bleachers with bad intentions.

I looked at Paul who was dumbfounded, his shoulders slunk

forward.

I was like, "It didn't work!" And Paul back pedaled toward me and said, "I see that."

The stampede was closing in fast, so I yelled, "What do we do now?" And Paul's eyes went wide like he was shell-shocked. I grabbed him by the shoulders and was like, "What do we do?" And finally he snapped out of it and said, "We… We run!"

But there was nowhere to run.

The zombies closed in from all directions.

Ep. 31: Bad News Part 2
Knighthood Never Looked So Good - 5,786 Views

Paul and I leaned against each other, back-to-back with Samwise at our feet, ready to fight and claw our way out—or at least I was.

I clenched my fist and reared back my leg when Paul said, "Don't!" And he must've sensed my confusion because he added, "Close your eyes instead!"

And then I knew what he had in mind.

Paul lifted his gaze to the burning encyclopedia and yelled, *"Kalah Kadoom!"*

Light erupted from the flames. Though my eyes were pinched shut, it was so bright it made my eyelids glow orange.

When I opened my eyes, the zombies had stumbled back and were rubbing their eyes. Mr. Brindle, releasing some colorful language I won't repeat here, disappeared into the crowd.

Paul grabbed my wrist and was like, "Let's get Usha and get out of here!"

We didn't have to search long for Usha. After we weaved our way through the horde of temporarily blinded zombies, having returned to her normal form, she met us as we exited through the gym doors. She immediately asked if the spell worked, explaining that she pulled her part of the spell off.

I told her nope as she joined us running down the hall. As Samwise darted between us and I leaped out of his way, I explained that Paul did his part, and she was like, "Then why didn't it work?" We made a sharp left turn and Paul answered, "I'm still trying to figure that out."

We made a right turn, sprinting down the main hallway leading to the parking lot, but two zombies waited by the doors. One of them adjusted his grip on a crowbar. I gulped and was like, "Let's try the back doors."

We turned back and made a left where we had made a right. The stampede of footfalls from the hallway gym made my heart pound even more. I picked up the pace and gestured to Paul and Usha, urging them on. But Paul stopped suddenly. "Wait!" he said. "You hear that?"

Usha and I halted too.

Samwise perked up, his ears pointing toward the ceiling, then let out a low growl

Over the sounds of the approaching zombies, we heard something.

"Help! Let me out! Help!"

We all looked back, and I was like, "The janitor's closet!" Pointing to a tire iron wedged into a door handle, Usha added, "They've locked someone in there." I think Paul recognized the voice because he got excited and said, "Not just anyone," as he yanked the tire iron out of the door handle.

The door opened and a younger looking teacher with shaggy hair and glasses fell out. He was sweaty and disheveled, and his loafers were scuffed at the tips. It appeared he'd been trying to break out for a long time.

When we saw him, Usha was like, "Mr. Macadoo?"

Then Mr. Macadoo climbed to his feet, seemingly dazed, and asked, "What is going on? All I did was turn down a donut from Mr. Brindle and he and some other teachers locked me in there."

The horde of zombies stormed around the corner and Paul was like, "I'll explain later. First, we have to get out of here."

Mr. Macadoo nodded and we took off in a sprint. The zombies drew closer as if we were prey to a pack of wolfhounds. We bounded through the hallways where the desks and chairs got smaller as the classrooms marched down from sixth grade to fourth grade, hoping to reach the rear exit. But to our dismay, the doors were locked shut with heavy chains.

Paul mumbled to himself and pulled on the chains. They weren't coming lose. Then Usha asked if there was a spell he could use, and Paul was like, "I... I don't know. I can look." And I nodded toward the end of the hall, where the first zombies lumbered into sight and told him, "You'd better hurry."

So Paul pulled the iPhone from his pocket, clicked on the app and began typing away. I noticed Mr. Macadoo's gaze narrowed on the iPhone. He looked befuddled.

"It's a grimoire," I said. "You know, a magic book." And Mr. Macadoo rubbed the back of his head, still looking confused.

Usha, who'd been watching our backs was like, "They're getting closer. Any luck?" Paul's fingers darted frantically across the iPhone's screen. He was trying.

The zombies were halfway down the hall. I clenched and unclenched my fists and said, "We're going to run out of time, Paul."

Then Mr. Macadoo ran to the nearest classroom door and offered an idea. "We can try a window!" he said.

I told him that all of the classrooms were locked but he insisted that one of them must be open. So we spread out and looked, checking the doors while Paul continued searching the grimoire. The closest doors to me were locked and Usha had no luck as well, but Mr. Macadoo found one that wasn't. He threw open the door and was like, "Here! Come in!"

Paul gave up searching the grimoire. He and Samwise dove through the open door behind me and Usha. Mr. Macadoo yanked it closed after us, then wedged a desk chair into the handle, bracing it shut. The first of the zombies slammed against it, causing it to shake violently. Samwise unleashed a flurry of barks.

Mr. Macadoo gestured to the window, telling us to climb out while he slowed the zombies down. And he didn't give us a chance to argue as he piled up desks in front of the door like it was an active shooter training session. Except they don't train us for active zombie attacks.

Paul cranked the window open and was like, "Ladies first," but I shoved him through the window, saying, "It's not a time for chivalry. Go!"

Paul climbed through and then called for Samwise to join him, but Samwise refused. He backed away, barking, so I picked him and handed him to Paul.

Usha climbed out next and I followed. I turned back to Mr. Macadoo, my hands on the window sill. His barricade was holding up. "Come on!" I said.

He shoved another desk onto the pile then scrambled out of the window. His stomach caught on the bottom edge of the window, tearing off a few buttons, but he was able to squeeze through. Then he was like, "Dang. We're in the courtyard." I nodded to the nearest of the courtyard's two exits and agreed, saying, "Yep. Let's hope one of the doors is unlocked."

Mr. Macadoo tried one door while me, Paul, Usha, and Samwise sprinted across the stone sidewalk and wet grass to the other one. I tried the handle. It was unlocked!

I started to open it and grabby zombie hands pushed through the gap. I kicked the door shut, smashing their fingers. An inhuman howl echoed from the other side before the door flung open. We stumbled back.

Mr. Macadoo toppled backward from his door, then scrambled to his feet as several zombies pushed it open. I shifted my attention to the window where we'd made our exit just as the first zombie squeezed herself through.

Usha cried out, "We're surrounded!" And the zombies edged in, their many weapons poised to strike. Samwise coiled up next to Paul, baring his teeth.

"What do we do?" I asked. And Mr. Macadoo, who placed himself between us and the zombies like he was a mother duck shielding her ducklings with her wing, shook his head and was like, "I don't know."

Then Paul bent down and picked up Samwise and said, "I think we surrender." Which caught us all off guard.

Usha was like, "You serious, Paul? What about Absalom's Key?" And Paul was like, "It's not my ideal decision but it will give me time to figure something out." Usha nodded her head and said, "Okay, but let's hope we don't end up mindless zombies. Or worse."

So we raised our hands like bank robbers giving up after a chase. The zombies wordlessly swooped in around us. Poking and prodding us, they herded us through the school and back to the gym where they shoved us into the cage where all the gym equipment is kept. Phil shut and locked the cage door, returning the key to the ring that dangled from a beltloop at his waist as he went back into the gym, leaving the equipment closet door open.

Mr. Brindle had yet to make an appearance, but we were certain they were acting under his accord.

Usha sank to a seated position against a rack of basketballs and commented that at least we weren't zombies. Yet.

"There's that," I agreed, sliding down beside her as I pulled out my phone which showed no signal. A complete dead zone. We couldn't even call for help. Usha noticed our signal-less predicament and was like, "Who would we call if we had service? Almost every adult in this town seems to be under Brindle's spell. My dad was out there."

Fighting off tears, Usha lowered her head into her arms. I wrapped my arm around her and squeezed her against my side. With a small whimper, Samwise curled up at her feet. Paul reached over and placed a hand on Usha's before removing it, then said, "We'll get him back. I promise."

Though Paul meant it, I couldn't see how it was possible.

After fiddling with the lock for a few minutes, Mr. Macadoo flipped over a bucket and took a seat. Wiping sweat off his forehead, he was like, "Okay, will one of you explain what's going on?"

I looked at Paul who went on to explain how catching Mr. Brindle trying to perform a spell in the woods behind the Swafford's old house, led him on an investigation where he discovered Mr. Brindle had turned our town into zombies.

And Mr. Macadoo was like, "So when Mr. Brindle offered me a donut, he was trying to steal a piece of my soul?" Paul nodded and Mr. Macadoo mused, "Wow. So a Keto cleanse saved my life."

We actually shared a short laugh, and then everyone went quiet.

Eventually Mr. Macadoo said, "Can I see it? The…"

"Grimoire," I said for him. And he nodded and was like, "Right. Right."

Paul pulled out the iPhone and clicked on the app and Mr. Macadoo gestured like this… and said, "May I?" and Paul handed it over.

Mr. Macadoo examined it, looking a little confused, saying, "This… looks just like an iPhone… but it's so much more. Isn't it?" Then his eyes blazed like Mr. Brindle's had as he added, "And… it's finally mine."

And Paul was like, "What?"

And I was like, "What?"

And Usha was like, "What?"

And Mr. Macadoo replied, "The Key… You gave it to me."

Ep. 32: Bad News Part 3
Knighthood Never Looked So Good - 6,899 Views

Paul crinkled his brow and was like, "Mr. Brindle?"

Mr. Macadoo's stood, his demeanor completely changed, was all, "Young Paul Weaver, you've been a worthy opponent. More clever than I expected. You saw through my unbreakable vow ruse, and I knew then it would take something truly unexpected to fool you."

Paul shot to a standing position and reached for the grimoire, but Mr. Macadoo blurted something that I think translated to "frozen feet," because that's what happened to our feet, they froze to the floor.

"What have you done with Mr. Macadoo?" Paul said, yanking on his knee as he struggled against his frozen feet.

Mr. Macadoo smirked and was like, "The question you should be asking is, what have I done with Mr. Brindle?"

Mr. Macadoo snapped his fingers and to our astonishment, a shimmer of light changed him into the old principal, who then said, "I mastered skin changing centuries ago. My grimoire may not be as powerful as the one you just gave me, but it does allow that."

And I was like, "Who... Who are you?" And he got this high and mighty posture and declared he was, "Sphire Macadon, student of Honorius of Thebes. But you know me better as Mr. Macadoo," before snapping his fingers again, reverting back to Mr. Macadoo.

Then Usha figured out what I hadn't quite come to yet. She said, "So that's why the spell didn't work earlier." And then Sphire—Mr. Macadoo—was like, "Very good, Usha. You attempted to steal Mr. Brindle's soul, but I'm not Mr. Brindle."

"So, you've been impersonating him this whole time?" I asked and he was like, "Not the whole time, only since he discovered my search for the hidden grimoire. I didn't want to hurt the old wizard, I only wanted to know where he was keeping it. But he was stubborn."

Then it clicked for Paul and he said, "So the night I got the grimoire, you were there in your Mr. Brindle skin to retrieve it." And Mr. Macadoo followed with, "And I would have if the old man's spell hadn't prevented me. Fortunately, you came along and grabbed it for me. You and your adorable little corgi weren't a part of my plan, but you proved useful. I guess you could say good things do come to those who wait. And I've waited a long time. Now, if you'll excuse me."

Then Mr. Macadoo whispered something to the lock and the door to the cage clicked open. He stepped through it, then locked it behind him. He peered at us through the fence and added, "I don't wish any of you any harm. And I regret that it has come to this. I really do."

So I was like, "If you regret it, then why are you doing it?" And he replied, "I made a promise. And I intend to keep it," before pulling out a gold necklace from the collar of his shirt and revealing a locket, which he opened, showing us the faded black and white image of a young woman.

Before either of us could question him further, our conversation was interrupted by a repeated sound approaching from the gym. A slow and methodical: *Clack. Clack. Clack.*

Mr. Macadoo's lips curled into a large grin. "Here she is."

The zombies had all dropped to a prone position, their faces against the floor as if worshiping the approaching visitor.

Slowly, a woman came into view. An old woman—and I mean great-grandma old. Her poofy white hair was stiff with hair spray, and she leaned on a walker with tennis balls covering the feet. She wore purple sweatpants and a pink sweater with a kitten on it.

Paul whispered, "I've met her before." He then went on to explain how they'd met at the nursing home where she'd helped him hide from Mr. Brindle, before he paused and was like "Come to think of it, I saw Mr. Macadoo there too."

Then Mr. Macadoo opened his arms and approached the woman, exclaiming, "I know it hasn't been long, but I've missed you!"

All the while Paul continued, talking more to himself than me and Usha. He was like, "That day I saw Mr. Macadoo at the nursing home, he wasn't there visiting his grandmother. He was visiting his—

And that's when Mr. Macadoo wrapped his arms around the old woman and kissed her passionately.

Yuck.

But the old woman pushed him away, snapping at him, "Do you have it? Tell me you have it." And Mr. Macadoo almost cowered away from her, linking his hands together as if pleading, he said, "Yes! Yes!"

"Let me see it, then!" she commanded, and he was like, "Right. Right," as he nervously pulled the iPhone out of his pocket and said, "I give you Absalom's Key."

The old woman's eyes lit up like she'd just scored in Bingo. As she took it in her hands, it changed into an old-timey diary. She whispered to herself, "After all these years."

Then Mr. Macadoo smiled warmly at her and was like, "Yes, my love." She then placed the grimoire into the walker's basket, lifted her gaze up to her lover, and asked, "Is the ritual ready?"

When she asked that, Mr. Macadoo bit down on his bottom lip and said, "Yes but…"

Then he trailed off.

Have you ever been talking to someone, and you know they want to say something, but they're afraid to say it, so they start looking at everything but you? Well, that was Mr. Macadoo right then.

Until the old woman snapped at him again: "But what?" And he shifted his weight from one leg to the other and said, "Are… Are all the souls of these villagers necessary?"

The old woman was obviously annoyed at his question. You could hear it in her voice when she said, "We discussed this already, Sphire. The wizard is too old, too out of touch with the power of the grimoire, so their souls will have to supplement. Unless…"

And that's when the old woman turned her attention to Paul, staring at him through her black cat-eye glasses.

She said, "Unless there is a younger wizard more in tune with the power of the grimoire."

My stomach knotted up. I looked over at Paul. The color drained from his face.

Mr. Macadoo stepped into the old woman's line of vision. "We can't do that," he said. "He's just a kid." But the old woman slammed the feet of the walker down like they were gavels and said, "That's never stopped me before," before adding, "You haven't gone soft on me, have you, Sphire?"

And Mr. Macadoo fingered the locket around his neck and was like, "No, but I love you the way you are. When I look into your eyes, I still see her face."

And the old woman snarled back, "But I don't. That locket is the last vestige of the youth that was stolen from me. When I gave that to you, you promised to help me undo the curse and get my vitality back. Or was that a lie?"

Then Mr. Macadoo was like, "I would never lie to you." And she snapped again, "Then fulfill your promise." Mr. Macadoo's expression dimmed, and he lowered his eyes and said, "Very well."

The old woman leaned on her walker wearing a very pleasant smile as if she'd just shared a slice of warm pie with a grandchild and was sending them home happy with a full belly.

Mr. Macadoo made a command and our feet unfroze, then a small horde of zombies filed in. They dragged us out to the gym floor kicking and screaming, leaving Samwise shut up and barking in the closet.

The zombies bound my and Usha's hands, gagged our mouths, then forced us into chairs underneath one of the basketball hoops. Paul, they forced to sit opposite an empty chair next to the altar at center court. The zombies who weren't standing guard, resumed their places in the bleachers, relighting their candles one by one like they were passing a treasured possession between them.

Soon the room was lit up with the candles' collective glow.

The old woman walked up to the altar, then stretched out her arms to the side. Mr. Macadoo, his head bent reverently, approached her from behind carrying a silky kimono. I couldn't be certain, but I thought I spotted a hint of regret in his downturned lips as he slipped the kimono over the old woman's arms.

Then the old woman commanded the other sacrifice be brought out and seconds later two zombies carried out someone from a nearby hallway, their feet dragging limply across the gym floor. The person's head was covered by a pillowcase, but I had a strong suspicion about who it was. And my suspicions were confirmed when they placed the person on the empty chair and removed the pillowcase.

Mr. Brindle—the real Mr. Brindle—sat with his eyes closed and head drooped. His clothes were disheveled, he was pale and thin and in need of a shave with patches of spiky gray hair covering his face and neck.

The old woman regarded her two sacrifices and when her gaze fell upon my brother, tears filled my eyes and I struggled against my bonds. My cries were stifled by the gag, becoming nothing but inaudible grunts lost under the chant that arose from the army of zombies in the bleachers.

The old woman gestured to Paul and Mr. Brindle and cried out, "With these two souls, I shall be youthful again!"

A cheer erupted from the zombies, and she was like, "Let the ritual begin!"

Another cheer.

I screamed again but nobody paid attention.

And for the first time, I saw genuine fear in my brother's face and I cringed so hard I felt like my chest was caving in on itself. I could do nothing but watch.

Mr. Macadoo approached the altar. He bowed his head and extended his hands, shouting a command in a language I couldn't understand.

Like lighting bugs summoned by the setting sun, the flames from the zombies' candles leaped from their candles and flew to center court, burying themselves in the stack of wood. The gym went dark for a second or two before *FLASH!* The altar burst to life with a pillar of flame but strangely no smoke.

Mr. Macadoo shouted another command and tendrils of fire split off the pillar, stretching in all directions across the gym, reigniting the zombies' candles. The room was fully aglow again and the tendrils returned to the altar.

Keeping his head bowed, Mr. Macadoo backed away. The chanting resumed and the old lady stepped forward and said, "Today, we undo a wrong. Today, what was stolen will be returned to me."

At this point the old woman began to chant. I don't know exactly what she said, but it sounded something like:

"Luvenis et vitale coom anime sequential. Dare et accipere. Obligata eos and me."

She started off low and slow but each time she repeated it, she picked up the volume and cadence.

The pillar of fire responded to her words in the way snakes do to a charmer, slithering from side to side in a strange kind of entrancing dance.

I found myself drawn to the fire's movements and change in color. Without making a sound, besides the soft crackling of the burning wood, the fire seemed to call to me—to everybody. And that's when I noticed Mr. Brindle.

I could tell the fire called to him too, but he was straining against it. He pinched his eyes shut and a vein throbbed in his neck. I glanced over at Paul, but it was too late for him. His eyes were wide open, staring at the flame.

I tried to scream at Paul to stop. I tried.

Usha tried too.

We both tried.

But…

Soon, a translucent mist with a strange glow began filtering out of Paul's eyes, draining into the flame.

Mr. Brindle's will gave way seconds later and he too peered into the dancing flame. His soul began leaving him soon after.

The fire shifted into a deep purple-reddish color for a moment as it absorbed the two souls, then smoke, as black as a starless night sky, poured from the flames. The old woman lifted her hands from the walker and tilting her head back, breathed in the smoke.

Almost instantly, puffs of white hair began falling out, with vibrant, darker hair sprouting in its place. The wrinkled skin of her face hardened and began to flake off, revealing fresh skin underneath. Her hips narrowed and she grew taller before my eyes.

The de-aging process was underway and Paul and Mr. Brindle were fading fast, becoming brittle like aged wood. Mr. Macadoo watched the scene unfold with his face scrunched up in what might have been a mixture of regret and horror.

There was little hope.

But I didn't consider the ingenuity and courage of Paul's most loyal friend.

Just as Paul's eyes started to close, Samwise burst through the gym closet doors. Somehow, he had found a way to let himself out.

Barking like mad, Samwise leaped on the nearest zombie to him, toppling the man over and creating a chain reaction that sent one side of the bleachers falling like dominoes. Multiple fires started. Gray smoke rose from the spreading flames as the zombies scrambled to put the fires out.

But they were too late. With a clanking of little used pipes, water rained down from the sprinklers overhead. The chanting stopped and the pillar of fire returned to a normal orange color then succumbed to the downpour. The woman's transformation ceased, leaving her mangled by age and youth.

"No! No! No!" she bellowed. "You hideous creature!"

Pointing a finger, she fired a bolt of purple electricity at Samwise. It missed him by inches, scorching the gym floor behind him.

She seethed and screamed at him, at the universe, "I only wanted what was stolen from me and you've ruined it!"

She fired again, but Samwise scampered out of the way. Zigzagging across the gym floor, Samwise was proving to be an elusive target.

At the same moment, the zombie guarding me bent down and to my utter surprise, untied my hands and feet before speaking.

"*I never wished you any harm,*" the zombie said with the same deep voice from before, "*Get your brother and run away before it's too late.*"

It took a moment for me to realize what was happening—that it was Mr. Macadoo controlling and speaking through the zombie. But I didn't waste time dwelling on it. I ripped the gag out of my mouth and went to work untying Usha. Once I got her out of the chair, I said, "You free Mr. Brindle and I'll get Paul."

After a minute or so, the sprinklers stopped, but they'd done their job and put out all the fires, freeing up the zombies to chase down Samwise.

While they and the old lady were distracted, Usha and I crept up to center court. I untied Paul who limply fell into my arms. He was exhausted and struggling to keep his eyes open.

"Wake up, Paul," I said. "We gotta get out of here."

And he was like, "But... the people."

Though he could only get out a few words, I knew what he meant. He didn't want to leave without freeing the zombies.

I was like, "Sorry, Paul. That will have to wait. We need to get out of here first." Though I promised we wouldn't leave without Samwise.

And that's when the old woman noticed us.

She snapped, "What do you think you're doing?" and fired a purple blast of electricity in our direction.

We didn't have time to dodge, so shielding Paul the best I could, I closed my eyes and braced for the blast.

But it didn't come.

I opened my eyes to see Mr. Macadoo fall to his knees in front of us, the purple energy radiating through him.

"What's this?" the old woman cried. And Mr. Macadoo climbed to his feet, his clothes sizzling. He grimaced and said, "I won't let you hurt them anymore."

But she was like, "They're standing in our way. It must be done."

But Mr. Macadoo wouldn't have it. He linked his hands together and pleaded, "No, Katalina, it doesn't. Please, stop this. I love you the way you are."

And she was like, "No, you don't. No one could." Then he was like, "I could and I do!"

Then she snarled and said, "I'm hideous." But he definitely didn't see her that way because he approached her saying, "Not to me, you're not. You're beautiful and always have been."

When Mr. Macadoo said that, the old woman looked down and he added softly, "Please, stop this, Katalina. Let them all go."

Her face still cast down, she said back, "My beauty was a good thing. I only want to be the woman in your locket again." And Mr. Macadoo untucked the locket from his collar and replied, "You are the good thing. Not this locket."

With those words, Mr. Macadoo ripped the locket off his neck, snapping the chain, and tossed it across the gym. The old woman reached longingly for it. "No!" she bellowed.

Mr. Macadoo stepped closer, took her hands in his and whispered, "That locket isn't necessary when I have you."

The old woman's gaze was still on the locket, and she was like, "You really think so?" Mr. Macadoo gently touched the old woman's chin, turning her head to face him. "Yes," he said.

Their eyes met and for a moment the anger in the old woman's face ebbed way. But then she must have caught a glimpse of her mangled reflection in Mr. Macadoo's glasses.

"You're lying," she snarled and squeezed Mr. Macadoo's hands. "I'm worse than hideous!"

I froze with shock as purple energy rippled from her hands

and into Mr. Macadoo. He let out a scream of agony and then vaporized away into nothing, leaving behind a pair of glasses sitting atop a steaming pile of clothes.

The old woman gasped with horror then cupped her face with her half-wrinkled hands, muttering to herself.

Samwise slithered out of the grasp of a zombie and finally found his way to Paul's side. Usha quickly joined us, telling us she'd got Mr. Brindle out of the gym.

"Good," I said, "let's get out of here." But Paul raised a hand in protest and said, "No. Not without… freeing the people."

I tried to…

I tried to argue with him, but he wouldn't listen. He said he had a plan then asked Usha if she still had the chalk. She told him yes and he said, "Get the locket. You'll know what to do after that."

Usha nodded knowingly and darted off, grabbing the locket and departing the gym. It took me a moment, but then I figured out Paul's plan.

Paul turned to me, grave faced, and said, "If this doesn't… doesn't work. Take care of Samwise for me."

Tears welled in my eyes as my heart sank into my stomach.

I was like, "Paul, you don't have to do this."

Even though the zombies had encircled us—waiting for the old woman's command—and Paul was pale and weak from the life the ritual had taken from him, I saw courage in his eyes.

He stood up straight and replied, "Yes, I do. I'm a Paladin Knight."

Behind him, the old woman pounded the tennis ball covered feet of the walker against the gym floor and howled, "This is all your fault. You ruined everything! I was supposed to be young again. Young!"

Paul turned to her. "You still can be," he said. "But only if you let my family and friends go." But she hissed at him, "You wish to bargain with me? What can you possibly offer?"

And Paul was like, "My soul. In exchange for their safety. You know it's enough to replenish your youth."

Then the old woman's eyes narrowed on him, and she said, "Your soul is a good thing. You'd give it up for them?" And Paul looked back at me and then down at Samwise who hadn't left his side and said, "Of course."

The old woman smiled with satisfaction. "Very well," she said. "I accept your gift. Your friends will go free once my transformation is complete."

Paul nodded.

Clapping her hands together, the old woman cackled then shouted out an incantation. Fire leaped from her palms onto the altar, where it smoldered for a few seconds before bursting into open flames.

I swallowed hard, not sure how Paul was going to pull it off.

The old woman closed her eyes and started chanting again, her cadence growing in volume and speed.

"Luvenis et vitale coom anime sequential. Dare et accipere. Obligata eos and me!"

"Luvenis et vitale coom anime sequential. Dare et accipere. Obligata eos and me!"

"Luvenis et vitale coom anime sequential. Dare et accipere. Obligata eos and me!"

The flame began its entrancing dance and shifted in color, from orange to blue before settling on the deep red. Once again, it drew my gaze though I tried to resist.

Paul, though, was ready.

He dropped his attention to Samwise and gestured to the old woman's walker. "See the tennis balls, Samwise?" he said. "Fetch."

Bending his head low, Samwise bolted around the altar, leaped up, and snagged the walker's basket in his teeth. Yanking back, Samwise pulled the walker over. It fell to the gym floor with a crash, breaking the old woman's concentration and spilling the contents of the basket over the hardwood.

Among them was the grimoire in diary form.

The old woman screamed and pointed her finger at Samwise, crying, "Not again!"

Purple energy sparked off her fingertips.

She roared, "Curses, you filthy mongrel! I'll finish you, yet!"

But her finger went limp as the purple energy evaporated into smoke. The old woman peered at her hand with confusion. She was like, "What's happening?"

At the same moment, Paul climbed to his feet holding the grimoire and said, "I'm happening."

The old woman snapped her attention to him, but her eyes widened with horror when the diary morphed back into the iPhone.

"You lied!" she roared. But Paul smirked through his pain and was like, "No. I offered you a gift and you accepted it."

Realization of what Paul was about to do hit the old woman like a stiff breeze. She glared and started to say, "You little—

But Paul countered with:

"Reponere senex dot com novum, Ray Romano filum, consuno et add!"

The soul shredder spell.

It worked!

The old woman threw her head back and howled in disgust as she vaporized into thin air from head to foot, leaving behind a pile of smoldering old lady's clothing.

At that moment, Samwise trundled up to Paul, a tennis ball in his mouth. Paul weakly reached down and patted him on the head and said, "Good boy," then…

Then he collapsed.

Ep. 33: Bad News Part 4
Knighthood Never Looked So Good - 7,143 Views

Sorry, everyone...

I had to stop recording because...

Because Paul's in a coma.

The doctors don't know what's going on—they've labeled him a medical mystery—but Mr. Brindle says he'll wake up.

As it turns out, Mr. Brindle was once a powerful wizard. According to him, there's a cost to every spell and the one Paul used to trap the old witch in her locket—the soul shredder spell—drained him near to death.

But I don't know if Mr. Brindle really believes Paul will wake up or if he's just telling Usha and me that to make us feel better.

I hope he's telling the truth.

I hope.

Although Mr. Brindle had given up the wizarding life, he summoned some of his old power to use the grimoire to free the zombies and return all the shreds of souls Mr. Macadoo and his lover, Katalina Usgesev, had stolen—once he'd retrieved his old ratty-bathrobe-looking cloak, of course.

The people under their spell are none the wiser. It's like they'd had their memories wiped by the device Will Smith used in that old movie *Men in Black*. However, I did hear one of Mom's friends tell her over the phone about a strange dream she had where she was chasing a corgi around the Middle school gym.

Speaking of Samwise, he hasn't left Paul's bedside, much to some of the hospital staff's consternation. He's a good boy.

And the grimoire? Technically, Absalom's Key belongs to Paul now. Though Mr. Brindle tried to destroy it that night in the woods behind the Swafford's old place, it found its way to Paul. And according to Mr. Brindle, Paul's fate will be forever entwined with the grimoire even if Paul should choose to never train to be a wizard—a particularly dangerous proposition.

But that only matters if Paul—

What was that?

Did you guys hear that? It sounded like.

Hold on sec.

Bark! Bark! Bark!

Samwise?

Samwise!

PAUL!!!!

Oh my gosh, guys! He's awake! He's home!

Ep. 34: Not A Paladin Knight After All.
Knighthood Never Looked So Good - 5,786 Views

Wow...

That was crazy.

I guess Ruth filled you guys in so I don't have to. I didn't watch the videos she posted yet, but I saw the comments. Your well wishes are appreciated.

It turns out there were a lot of people praying and rooting for me. I got this huge get-well card signed by everyone in the sixth grade. Even the sisters of Medusa signed it.

Though I was asleep and couldn't remember it, Hurston stopped by several times, and we're supposed to hang out soon. We're going to see a movie or go to the mall. I told him to invite the new kid too.

Usha stopped by as well when she wasn't playing tennis. She wrote me a note. I'm not going to tell you what it says and no, I'm not blushing. My cheeks are just red from...

The excitement of...

Making another video! Yeah!

Anyway, things with her dad have improved slightly, at least that's the impression I got. She thanked me for saving her dad, but she was just as heroic as me. I mean, I couldn't have done the spell without her.

And I guess that brings me to the question you all keep asking in the comments.

Where do babies come from?

Ha. Ha. Just kidding.

The real question you all keep asking is, am I going to train to be a wizard?

The answer is...

I don't know.

I'm going to give it some thought, but before that Samwise and I have a visit to make. A certain pappaw I know will love to hear about everything that happened, especially the courage of a certain corgi. Ain't that right, boy?

Bark!

And even if Pappaw's having a bad day and doesn't want to talk, it will still be worth the trip.

That's all I've got right now, so see you next time.

This is Paladin Knight Paul Weaver signing off.

Let's go, Samwise.

Bark!

The End

Acknowledgements

Publishing a book is a mighty endeavor—almost like carrying a magical ring to its fiery demise. And like Frodo, I couldn't have done it alone. There are many in the fellowship who helped me in this journey. I want to start first by giving thanks to my lord and savior Jesus Christ. Secondly, I want to thank my wife for her love, patience, and unending support. My daughters for keeping me humble and my son for igniting my imagination. I want to thank my parents for always taking my dreams seriously and my brother and sisters for their encouragement every step of the way. But also so many of my friends who've cheered me on, listened to my zany ideas, or offered words of encouragement.

Speaking of friends, I'm so grateful for my oldest friend, Kyle. When the team at Artemesia said they wanted illustrations, one artist came to mind. I knew Kyle would do phenomenal work, but his illustrations went beyond my expectations. Much of the success of this book belongs to him and it's been a pleasure and a privilege to collaborate on the visuals of this novel. Perhaps, one day we will get to work on our dream Star Wars project (hit us up, Lucasfilm), but until then, know that I truly valued every second we spent bringing Paul and Samwise's adventures to life.

A special thanks goes to my first readers Carol, Clara, and Lucy. Your input made this story better.

I would be remiss if I didn't mention Geoff and the team at Artemesia. Thanks for believing in Paul's story and for all of the hard work you did and continue to do behind the scenes. A special shoutout goes to my editor, Lisa, for her encouragement and careful work.

Finally, I want to thank the librarians who shelve this book, the booksellers who carry this book (especially my favorite hometown bookstore, Star City Booksellers) and the many of you who read and shared Paul and Samwise's story with others.

God bless!

S.C. McMurray

About the Author

S. C. McMurray grew up on the mean rural roads of southwestern Ohio where he honed his storytelling skills on anyone willing to listen. Now he does it professionally as an author and teacher. Sean still lives in rural Ohio with the love of his life and his favorite audience, their three not-so-little children.